Anonymous

A History of the Family and Descendants of John Collin

Cyclopedia of Biography

Anonymous

A History of the Family and Descendants of John Collin
Cyclopedia of Biography

ISBN/EAN: 9783337098346

Printed in Europe, USA, Canada, Australia, Japan

Cover: Foto ©Raphael Reischuk / pixelio.de

More available books at **www.hansebooks.com**

CYCLOPEDIA OF BIOGRAPHY,

CONTAINING A

HISTORY OF THE FAMILY AND DESCENDANTS

OF

JOHN COLLIN,

A

FORMER RESIDENT OF MILFORD, CONN.,

TO WHICH

IS APPENDED A NOTICE OF THEIR KINDRED, NEAR AND
REMOTE, BY BLOOD AND AFFINITY.

———

HUDSON:
M. P. WILLIAMS, REGISTER AND GAZETTE OFFICE.
1872.

CYCLOPEDIA OF BIOGRAPHY

OF

JOHN COLLIN.

————•◆•————

THE Rev. WILLIAM SCRIBNER, in his historical comments upon the French nation, says :

" The prodigious exodus of the French people which followed the revocation of the edict of Nantes, constitutes one of the most important historical events of the seventeenth century. Many of the French people were driven to expatriate themselves in the persecutions of 1715, 1724 and 1744. They settled in nearly all the countries of Europe ; and there was not a country which received them which they did not enrich. There is no computing how much of her prosperity England owes to the great waves of population which flowed over to her from France in those times. They were skilled, intelligent and laborious, and they were among the most virtuous people of the world."

Among those whom those persecutions drove to expatriation was John Collin, born in France in 1706. Emigrating to this country he settled at Milford, New Haven county, Connecticut. Having received a nautical education, in which he acquired a knowledge of the English language, he was placed in command of the ship Swan, belonging to John Merwin, whose daughter, Hannah, he subsequently married, and by whom he had three sons :

John, born July 15th, 1732.
David, born February 18th, 1734.
James, born 1736.

He continued in command of the ship for sixteen years. But in 1746, having sailed from Milford Haven for the West Indies, he, with the ship, was lost at sea. His family waited his return in painful suspense till time demonstrated that he never could return :

> "The moon had twelve times changed her form,
>   From glowing orb to crescent wan,
> Midst skies of calm and scowl of storm,
>   Since from the port that ship had gone.
> But ocean keeps her secrets well,
>   And now is known that all is o'er,
> No eye hath seen, no tongue can tell
>   His fate; he ne'er was heard of more."

His papers and books, now preserved among his kindred, show that he was a good penman, and an accomplished scholar. And they have erected to his memory a granite monument in the grounds of the Hillsdale Rural Cemetery Association.

JOHN COLLIN, son of John and Hannah Merwin Collin, was born in Milford, Conn., July 15th, 1732. Having lost his father in his infancy, his maternal grandfather, John Merwin, became his guardian, and he taught him to pursue those moral, prudential and industrial habits by which he subsequently acquired wealth and distinction.

He married Sarah Arnold of Dutchess county, N. Y., September 16th, 1758, by whom he had three children :

Anthony, born February 24th, 1760.
Hannah, born June 7th, 1763.
John, born September 19th, 1772.

His wife, Sarah, having died December 29th, 1791, he married Deidama Morse Davidson, May 13th, 1792. He died in Hillsdale, August 21st, 1809.

In 1773 he received a captain's commission from Governor Tryon, the British colonial Governor, and in 1777 he received a captain's commission from George Clinton, the Governor of the State of New York.

He possessed great physical strength and mechanical ingenuity, and he was a prominent actor in the public enterprises of the day.

He was baptized in the Congregational Church, in Milford, May 16th, 1736, and was ever very steadfast in his religious opinions, and is said to have manifested much ability in their defence. He was also a member of the Masonic fraternity.

He was cotemporary with Alexander Hamilton, William W. Van Ness, Elisha Williams and Jacob Rutsen Van Rensselaer, and his papers show that he was on terms of friendly intimacy with them, rendering to and receiving from them reciprocal favors.

DAVID COLLIN, son of John and Hannah Merwin Collin, born in Milford, Conn., February 19th, 1734. Having lost his father in his infancy, he became the ward of John Merwin, his maternal grandfather, through whom he acquired the habits of industry and economy by which he obtained great wealth. He married Lucy Smith, of Dutchess county, N. Y., February 19th, 1764, by whom he had two children :

Hannah, born 1765.
David, born February 22d, 1767.

His wife, Lucy, having died March 15th, 1767, he married Esther Gellett January 19th, 1772, by whom he had three children :

Lucy, born February 28th, 1773.
Sally, born 1775.
James, born April 5th, 1777.

He had been a lieutenant in the British army during the French war, and was present at an unsuccessful attack upon

Fort Ticonderoga. During the war of the American Revolution his house was plundered by a band of robbers, who treated his family with great rudeness, and tortured him nearly to the verge of life. He died December 17th, 1818, and his wife, Esther, died May 8th, 1824. He had been baptized in the First Congregational Church of Milford, May 16th, 1736.

JAMES COLLIN, son of John and Hannah Merwin Collin, born in Milford, Conn., and baptized in the First Congregational Church of that town, October 30th, 1737, and died in his infancy. His mother had become a member of the Congregational Church on the 16th of May, 1735.

ANTHONY COLLIN, son of John and Sarah Arnold Collin, born in Dutchess county, N. Y., February 24th, 1760, was a soldier in the war of the American Revolution, and was made a prisoner by the army of Sir Henry Clinton, October 16th, 1777, and died in captivity in December following.

HANNAH COLLIN, daughter of John and Sarah Arnold Collin, born in Dutchess county, N. Y., June 7th, 1763, and married Thomas Truesdell, October, 8th, 1781; died in Hillsdale, June 26th, 1817. They had six children:

John W., born May 7th, 1783.
Sarah, born June 17th, 1785.
Harry, born March 1st, 1788.
Beebe, born January 10th, 1794.
Arnold, born September 16th, 1796.
Gove, born May 14th, 1802.

JOHN COLLIN, son of John and Sarah Arnold Collin, born in Dutchess county, N. Y., September 19th, 1772, and married Ruth Holman Johnson, October 23d, 1798; died in Hillsdale, December 28th, 1833. They had nine children:

James, born January 16th, 1800.

John Francis, born April 30th, 1802.

Sarah Amanda, born April 21st, 1804.

Jane Miranda, born February 14th, 1807.

Hannah, born December 19th, 1809.

Ruth Maria, born March 1st, 1813; died June, 1838.

Henry Augustus, born January 6th, 1817.

William Quincy, born November 23d, 1819; died July 30th, 1822.

Clynthia A., born December 10th, 1822; died August 5th, 1828.

James Collin, son of John and Ruth Holman Collin, born January 16th, 1800, and married to Jane B. Hunt, of Lenox, Mass., May 5th, 1822, by whom he had three children:

James Hunt, born March 21st, 1823.

Jane Sophia, born November 27th, 1824.

John Francis, born February 15th, 1827; died same year.

His wife, Jane B., having died February 25th, 1827, he married Velona Hill, of Hillsdale, March 17th, 1828, by whom he had six children:

Ellen H., born February 20th, 1829.

Charles R., born March 1st, 1832.

Louis E., born August 10th, 1833.

John H., born February 25th, 1835.

Mary C., born March 15th, 1838.

William M., born March 23d, 1842.

His wife, Velona, died August 11th, 1846, and he married Chastine Wolverton, of Albany, N. Y., September 7th, 1847, by whom he had six children:

Edwin W., born September 19th, 1849.

Mortimer and Monteath, twins, born December 9th, 1852.

George W., born December 13th, 1855.
Hattie May, born May 1st, 1856.
Lizzie A., born March 12th, 1860.

Very early in years he commenced business as a merchant in North Egremont, Mass., but subsequently engaged in the furnace business at Lenox, Mass., in which he continued for many years and finally added to that business the manufacture of plate glass, at which he continued till his death, which occurred December 16th, 1861.

He was an accomplished business man and distinguished for industry, intelligence and high moral and social characteristics.

JOHN FRANCIS COLLIN, son of John and Ruth Holman Johnson Collin, born in Hillsdale, April 30th, 1802, and married Pamelia Jane Tullar, daughter of Charles and Rebecca Race Tullar, of Egremont, Mass., September 23d, 1827, by whom he had six children.

Jane Paulina, born 1828; died September 17th, 1830.
Hannah Clynthia, born 1829; died March 14th, 1831.
Pamelia Laurania, born 1831.
John Frederick, born 1833.
Quincy Johnson, born 1836.
Frances Amelia, born 1840.

His wife Pamelia having died June 8th, 1870, he married Jane Becker, daughter of Philip and Elizabeth De Groff Becker, of Hillsdale, January 16th, 1871.

His birth occurred about eighteen years after the close of the American Revolutionary war. In his boyhood he had listened to the historic incidents of that war from those who had acted in or been sufferers by it. He had listened to those relations from the lips of his maternal grandmother, and but few possessed so interesting colloquial powers as she. She told of her brother James importing arms and munitions of war from France, and of his sagacity in avoiding British cruisers which thronged the coasts of Massachusetts. She told of the painful interest felt by herself and family while listening to the battle of Bunker Hill, in which her brothers James, Bartlet and Watson were engaged. She told of the parting scene with her brother Abner, the packing of his clothes in his knapsack by maternal hands, and the last embrace, as he, only sixteen years of age, went forth with Capt. Jacob Allen's Bridgwater company to aid in opposing the army of Gen. Burgoyne. She described the scene in the family when the letter from her brother James brought the information that Abner had fallen in battle.

The death of Anthony Collin, too, had excited a deep interest. Only sixteen years of age, he had been made prisoner by the army of Sir Henry Clinton, and suffered and died in captivity, and his mother went to her grave with a broken heart.

Under these circumstances it is not strange that John F. Collin, in his boyhood, imbibed a hatred to the British name, and that the incidents in the war of 1812 should have given him strong democratic proclivities.

Being physically strong and healthy in his youth, while his older brother was the reverse, his father resolved to bring him up to be his successor on the farm. To that end he employed him during summer on the farm, and during winter in procuring an education. The effect of his early agricultural training has produced the fruits of a successful agricultural life. And that his time was not wasted as a student, may be inferred from the following penegyric of his old preceptor:

Dear Sir—It becomes my duty at the close of the term, to write you a few lines on the subject of your son Francis. He has distinguished himself the past term by his manly and correct deportment as a gentleman, and by his application and success as a scholar. He seems to have laid the foundation for a correct knowledge of the Latin language, and to have opened his mind to the reception of those liberal sciences in which he seems destined to be distinguished. While he is one of the brightest ornaments of our academy, he is dear to our school and village.

Sincerely and respectfully yours,

LEVI GUASON.

To Mr. John Collin.

The term thus alluded to by Mr. Guason, proved to be the last of his life as a student. His father's feeble health made his services indispensable at home, and though in his minority, his father devolved upon him all his out-business, which extended over much of the State, and involved much litigation. He also employed him in the settlement of the mercantile business of his elder brother, which had become very much embarrassed. During the years devoted to this latter object, he made the acquaintance and married Miss Pamelia Jane Tullar, whose head to advise and hand to assist and heart to cheer, has contributed very much to his success in life.

He had given much attention to the political history of his country, and became enthusiastically attached to its institutions. He considered the religious influence of the clergy, one of the strongest pillars of the State, so long as that influence was reflex rather than direct. But a political clergy, while corrupting the church, he believed to be not only dangerous to liberty, but mischievious to all civil institutions, of which the Jesuits were an example. Political clergymen had brought all martyrs to the torture. And political clergymen had expatriated both his paternal and maternal ancestors from their native countries, and compelled them to make this their country by adoption. He saw with regret and alarm, legislation introduced initiatory to that great evil, in the Rev. Joshua Leavitt's recommended Christian party in politics.

Influenced by these considerations, on the 13th of February, 1830, he addressed a meeting at the Baptist Church in Hillsdale Center, at which the Hon. Henry Loop presided, and David G. Wooden acted as secretary. That address was published and attracted some attention, and a venerable politician tendered him his mantle. Another from an exceeding high mountain showed him the kingdoms of the earth and the glory of them.

But ties of friendship, nor the allurements of ambition, could divest him of the prejudices of youth and the convictions of maturer years, and he cast his lot with the democracy of the country.

In 1833 he received the Democratic nomination to the State Legislature, and was elected by 800 majority in the county, having received 207 majority in his native town. In that year his father died, having, by his will, imposed upon him the settlement of his estate and the execution of many trusts.

He was soon after appointed a commissioner to settle controversies between the Hudson and Berkshire railroad company and certain individuals over whose premises the road was required to run. In 1837, and for seven successive years, he was elected supervisor in the town of Hillsdale.

He was a delegate to the Congressional Convention which gave Robert McClellan his first nomination to Congress, and when the tariff act of 1842 was under consideration, Mr. McClellan sent him a draft of the bill and wished his opinion on it; and he signified to Mr. McClellan his unqualified disapprobation of it, for it interfered with the reserved rights of States. It interfered with the industrial interests of persons within States, giving some persons great privileges at the expense of others. It gave to certain States privileges at the expense of others. It disturbed the natural laws of trade. It sought to circumvent the edicts of the Almighty by enabling, by special legislation, a privileged class of citizens to earn their bread by

the sweat of others' brows. It was deceptive in its provisions. Its minimums and certain other of its provisions
were misnomers. To deceive the public, it fixed fictitious,
extravagantly advanced valuations upon certain imports,
and upon those advanced valuations imposed advalorem
duties, and under the pretense of protection to the home
manufacturer it imposed deceptive duties upon articles of
most general use at home, and such as the manufacturers
themselves were then successfully competing in markets
with the manufacturers of other countries. In fine, he considered that tariff a dangerous precedent and a great moral
wrong. But notwithstanding all these objections it became
a law.

In 1844 he was elected to Congress himself. His strong
convictions of the impolicy of the tariff of 1842, led him to
make great exertions for its repeal, and it was repealed.
And the committee of ways and means allowed him to dic-
tate many of the provisions in the act of 1846.

It was one of his principles of political economy, that
wealth obtained by industry and prudence is a source of
national greatness, strength and happiness; but when obtained by other means was a source of national weakness,
corruption and misery.

Even a desire to obtain wealth by other means than industry and prudence has in it the root of all evil.

It was under the influence of such principles that the
tariff act of 1846 was conceived, and the ten years succeeding its passage may be claimed to have been the
halcyon age of the republic.

That tariff produced an ample revenue for an economi-
cal government.

Its burthens were imposed equally upon all, and left
each and all to the full enjoyment of their own industry
and economy.

The wicked and odious laws which had bestowed bounties upon Boston rum and other New England commodities, were beginning to be erased from our statute books.

The sovereignty of States over all their internal and municipal interests was fully recognized.

Not a fort had been erected upon the territory of a State without having first obtained the consent of such State for its erection, the State reserving to itself sovereignty over such fort, except for the sole purpose of defence against external aggression.

Not a federal bayonet was allowed to interfere within the limits of a State, even in case of insurrection, till invited by the authority of the State itself. Nor had the federal courts a right to adjudicate where the issues were entirely between citizens of the same State.

The whole prerogative of the general government was confined to the external interests of States, and to their defence, and to their intercourse with each other and with foreign States. And like the sun reflecting its beneficence upon its satellites, and by its attraction keeping them within their orbits, and while independent of each other, preventing collisions.

During the eventful ten years succeeding 1846, all that was great and good in this nation flourished; the people were peaceful, prosperous and happy, and the nation raised from a state of mediocrity to be one of the mightiest of the world. Even Europe profited by our example of State sovereignty, and Portugal, Holland, Belgium, Sweden, Denmark, Switzerland and Greece, with populations no larger than our individual States, were recognized as competent for self-government, and were sovereign over their own interests. And the greater sovereignties of Europe protected them in that sovereignty.

But the influences which conceived such laws as the tariff act of 1842, had produced the imputed cause which formed the excuse for provoking our late civil war. Under the excitement of that war, amendments have been made to the federal constitution, in each of which are insidious provisions, revolutionary, depriving not only the States but the federal courts of their prerogatives, and vesting them in the discretion of Congress.

The consequence of all this is, that crime pervades our land. And corruption, instead of being exceptional, is the rule among all in official positions. Even the ermine of our highest courts has become soiled. The legal tender decision must impair our credit, and leave an unfavorable impression in respect to us among all enlightened nations.

A subsidized press and pensioned editors are lavishing their sophistry upon the people, and to effect their purposes they show alike their editorial and pictorial buffoonry upon the good and the bad, the knave and the patriot.

Under these influences and wicked legislation, the wealth of this nation is rapidly becoming concentrated in the hands of knavish individuals or soulless corporations, and the people are imperceptibly gliding into a state of slavery. And instead of being, as in times past, the pride of nations and the hope of the world, civilization is looking upon us with pity and contempt.

Notwithstanding seven years of peace, the mailed hand of the conquerer has still got by the throat the people of many of our States, and is feeling its way to those of others, and Federal bayonets have already gleamed to overawe our northern elections, the most important of our franchise.

The only hope to the friends of freedom is in that God whose ways are so far above human comprehension. He may be chastising us for our good, for—

> He moves in a mysterious way,
> His wonders to perform,
> He plants his footsteps on the sea,
> And rides upon the storm.

SARAH AMANDA COLLIN, daughter of John and Ruth Holman Johnson Collin, born in Hillsdale, April 21st, 1804, and married to Rodney Hill, son of Jonathan and Christine E. Wilcox Hill, of Hillsdale, February 20th, 1825; died in Great Barrington, 1867. They have had two children:

John Henry, born May 16th, 1826.
Ruth Maria, born January 23d, 1829.

JANE MIRANDA COLLIN, daughter of John and Ruth Holman Collin, born in Hillsdale, February 14th, 1807, and married to Rev. Hiram H. White, of Canton, Conn., June 2d, 1830.

HANNAH COLLIN, daughter of John and Ruth Holman Johnson Collin, born in Hillsdale, December 19th, 1809, and married Lewis Wright, of Xenia, Ohio, April 16th 1833, by whom she had one daughter:

Melinda T., born in Wilmington, Ohio, March 27th 1834.

RUTH MARIA COLLIN, daughter of John and Ruth Holman Johnson Collin, born in Hillsdale, March 1st, 1813; died June, 1838.

HENRY AUGUSTUS COLLIN, son of John and Ruth Holman Johnson Collin, born in Hillsdale, January 6th, 1817, and married Sarah Ann White, of Sharon, Conn., October 29th, 1836, by whom he has had three children :

Henry Alonzo, born August 14th, 1837.
Sarah Adaline, born January 3d, 1840.
Edwin, born August 31st, 1842.

He was five times elected supervisor of the town of Hillsdale, and was highly respected for intelligence and integrity. In 1856 he moved to Mount Vernon, Linn county, Iowa.

WILLIAM QUINCY COLLIN, son of John and Ruth Holman Johnson Collin, born in Hillsdale, November 23d, 1819; died July 30th, 1822.

CLYNTHIA A. COLLIN, daughter of John and Ruth Holman Johnson Collin, born December 10th, 1822; died August 5th, 1828.

JAMES H. COLLIN, son of James and Jane B. Hunt Collin, born at Egremont, Massachusetts, March 21st, 1823, and married to Mary Elizabeth Wright, daughter of Lewis and Hannah Springer Wright, of Xenia, Ohio, July 12th, 1843, by whom he has had five children:

> Frances M., born August 3d, 1844.
> Sarah M., born November 5th, 1847.
> Emma S., born March 26th, 1850.
> Henry Clay, born November 27th, 1851.
> Jennie L., born September 11th, 1859.

JANE S. COLLIN, daughter of James and Jane B. Hunt Collin, born at Egremont, November 27th, 1824, and married to George Robbins, of Lenox, Mass., October 28th, 1847, by whom she has had two children:

> Mary E., born in Ohio.
> James, born in New Marlborough, Mass.

ELLEN H. COLLIN, daughter of James and Velona Hill Collin, born in Lee, Mass., July 20th, 1829, and married to Roswell Derbyshire, of Lenox, Mass., May 9th, 1849, and upon his decease she married H. Hills, May, 1854, by whom she has had two sons and one daughter, and is now living in Janesville, Rock county, Wisconsin.

CHARLES R. COLLIN, son of James and Velona Hill Collin, born at Lee, Mass., March 1st, 1832, and married Hannah Wilcox, of Elgin, Illinois, 1854, by whom he has four boys, and he is now a merchant in the State of Iowa.

LOUIS E. COLLIN, son of James and Velona Hill Collin, born at Lee, Mass., August 10th, 1833, and married Mary A. Macy, of Milwaukee, Wisconsin, by whom he has one son. He now resides in Chicago, Illinois.

JOHN H. COLLIN, son of James and Velona Hill Collin, born at Lee, Mass., February 25th, 1835, and is now living in the State of Iowa.

MARY C. COLLIN, daughter of James and Velona Hill Collin, born at Lenox, Mass., March 15th, 1838, and married Lorezo L. Crowns, December 27th, 1859, by whom she has two sons and is now residing in Washington, in the District of Columbia.

WILLIAM M. COLLIN, son of James and Velona Hill Collin, born at Lenox, Mass., March 23d, 1842, and married Clara Rogers, daughter of the Hon. Charles Rogers, of Washington county, N. Y., 1869, and is now the cashier of the First National Bank of Sandy Hill, N. Y.

EDWIN W. COLLIN, son of James and Chastine E. Wolverton Collin, born at Lenox, September 19th, 1849, died at Pittsfield, Mass., 1871.

MORTIMER and MONTEATH COLLIN, twins, born December 9th, 1852.

GEORGE W. COLLIN, born December 13th, 1835.

HATTIE MAY COLLIN, born May 1st, 1858.

LIZZIE A. COLLIN, born March 12th, 1860.

All children of James and Chastine Wolverton Collin, and all in their infancy, are residing with their mother in Pittsfield, Mass.

FRANCES M. COLLIN, born August 3d, 1844.

SARAH M. COLLIN, born November 5th, 1847.

EMMA S. COLLIN, born March 26th, 1850.

HENRY CLAY COLLIN, born November 27th, 1851.

JENNIE L. COLLIN, born September 11th, 1859.

All children of James H. and Mary Elizabeth Wright Collin, are residing with their parents in Pittsfield, Mass.

JOHN FRANCIS COLLIN, son of James and Jane B. Hunt Collin, born in Egremont, Mass., February 15th, 1827, died April 9th, 1827.

PAMELIA LAURANIA COLLIN, daughter of John Francis and Pamelia Jane Tullar Collin, born in Hillsdale, December 12th, 1831, and married to the Rev. John Braden, of Xenia, Ohio, October 16th, 1856, by whom she has had three children :

Mary Eliza, born August 11th, 1858.

Francis Collin, born August 11th, 1860; died July 20th, 1861.

Fannie, born June 23d, 1866; died September 18th, 1866.

She now resides in Nashville, in the State of Tennessee.

JOHN FREDERICK COLLIN, son of John Francis and Pamelia J. Tullar Collin, born in Hillsdale, September 24th, 1833, and married Jennett Van Dusen, daughter of Seymour and Caroline McArthur Van Dusen, December 15th, 1857, by whom he has had three children :

John Jay, born December 12th, 1858; died July 2d, 1861.

Ruth Anna, born February 4th, 1863; died October 16th, 1870.

Frances Pamelia, born August 13th, 1866.

QUINCY JOHNSON COLLIN, son of John Francis and Pamelia Jane Tullar Collin, born in Hillsdale, August 20th, 1836, graduated at the Wesleyan University in Middletown, Conn., 1856, and married Martha Collin, daughter of Solomon Bingham and Julia Ann Bushnell Collin, March 28th, 1860, by whom he has had three children :

Carrie Louise, born January 14th. 1862.

May Amelia, born May 15th, 1865; died March 18th, 1869.

Grace Adelia, born July 19th, 1868.

He is now a clergyman, and is the pastor of a church in Washington street, Poughkeepsie, N. Y.

FRANCES AMELIA COLLIN, daughter of John Francis and Pamelia J. Tullar Collin, born in Hillsdale, December 12th, 1840, and married Sylvester Barbour, Esq., November 27th, 1860, by whom she has had four children :

Lizzie Lawrence, born September 21st, 1861.

Collin Henry, born July 6th, 1863.

Edward Humphry, born 1867 ; died February 13th, 1869.

Amy Louise, born September 25th, 1869.

She is now a resident of Ansonia, New Haven county, Conn.

HENRY ALONZO COLLIN, son of Henry Augustus and Sarah Ann White Collin, born in Hillsdale, August 14th, 1837, graduated at the Wesleyan University at Middletown, Conn., 1868, and married Cloe Matson, of Indiana, June 30th, 1868, by whom he has one child, born 1869. He now resides in Mount Vernon, Linn county, Iowa, and is a professor in Cornell College in that town.

SARAH ADALINE COLLIN, daughter of Henry Augustus and Sarah Ann White Collin, born in Hillsdale, January

3d, 1840, and married the Rev. James H. Golruth, a member of the Iowa Conference of the Methodist Episcopal Church, June 20th, 1869, by whom she has a daughter born March 1st, 1870.

EDWIN COLLIN, son of Henry Augustus and Sarah Ann White Collin, born in Hillsdale, August 31st, 1842. He spent some years as vice consul in Europe, and is now an attorney in the State of Iowa.

DAVID COLLIN, son of David and Lucy Smith Collin, born at Amenia, Dutchess county, N. Y., February 22d, 1767, and married Lucy Bingham, March 27th, 1791; died at Fayetteville, N. Y., June 2d, 1844. His children were :

> Harry, born March 15th, 1792.
> Lucy, born June 27th, 1796.
> David, born April 23d, 1794.
> Harriet, born February 9th, 1799.
> Lee, born February 14th, 1801.
> Hannah, born October 2d, 1803.
> Solomon Bingham, born March 7th, 1806.
> Amanda, born February 18th, 1809.
> Norton Smith, born July 24th, 1812.

HARRY COLLIN, son of David and Lucy Bingham Collin, born in Amenia, Dutchess county, N. Y., March 15th, 1792, and married Nancy McAlpin, of Hillsdale, April 2d, 1814; died October 8th, 1835. His children were :

> Harriet Ann, born October 28th, 1816.
> Henry Clark, born September 2d, 1818.
> Emeline, born September 6th, 1822.

HARRIET ANN COLLIN, daughter of Harry and Nancy McAlpin Collin, born in Benton, Yates county, N. Y., October 28th, 1816, and married Alfred Gilbert Bidwell, of Hillsdale, May 2d, 1837, by whom she has had seven children :

Florine Alfrett, born August 28th, 1839.
Nancy Jane, born April 7th, 1841.
Henry Collin, born June 11th, 1843.
Harriet Augusta, born October 7th, 1846.
Horace Gilbert, born May 24th, 1849.
Alfred Edgar, born November 27th, 1852.
William Welch, born November 28th, 1857.

HENRY CLARK COLLIN, son of Harry and Nancy McAlpin Collin, born in Benton, Yates county, N. Y., September 2d, 1818, and married Maria Louise Park, of Burlington, Otsego county, N. Y., September 23d, 1842, by whom he has had eight children:

Henry Park, born July 26th, 1843.
Charles Avery, born May 18th, 1846.
Mary Louise, born June 7th, 1848.
Frederick, born August 2d, 1850.
Emeline, born February 16th, 1852.
George, born February 3d, 1854.
William Welch, born January 2d, 1856.
Frank McAlpin, born September 17th, 1859.

EMELINE COLLIN, daughter of Harry and Nancy McAlpin Collin, born in Benton, Yates county, N. Y., September 6th, 1852, married William Wickham Welch, of Norfolk, Conn., November 7th, 1844 ; died October 29th, 1850. Her children were :

Emeline Alice, born May 13th, 1847.
William Henry, born April 8th, 1850.

HENRY PARK COLLIN, son of Henry Clark and Maria Louise Park Collin, born in Benton, N. Y., July 26th, 1843, graduated at Yale College, Conn., 1865, and also graduated

at the Union Theological Seminary in the city of New
York, 1869, and preached one year at Seymour, Conn., and
resigned his charge for the purpose of going to Germany:

CHARLES AVERY COLLIN, son of Henry Clark and Maria
Louise Park Collin, born in Benton, N. Y., May 18th,
1846, and graduated at Yale College, Conn., 1866. Having studied law, was admitted to the bar in the Spring of
1870, and in August of that year settled in Elmira, N. Y.,
and is now one of the law firm of Collin & Atwill.

MARY LOUISE, daughter of Henry Clark and Maria
Louise Collin, born at Benton, N. Y., June 7th, 1848, and
graduated at the Packard Collegiate Institute, Brooklyn,
N. Y., in 1867, and married to James Sanford Sears of
Geneva, N. Y., June 15th, 1870, at which place she now
resides.

FREDERICK COLLIN, son of Henry Clark and Maria
Louise Park Collin, born in Benton, N.Y., August 2d, 1850,
and graduated at Yale College, Conn., in 1871.

EMELINE COLLIN, daughter of Henry Clark and Maria
Louise Park Collin, born in Benton, N. Y., February 16th,
1852, and entered the Packard Collegiate Institute, Brooklyn, N. Y., September, 1869, at which place she is now
pursuing her studies, in 1871.

DAVID COLLIN, son of David and Lucy Bingham Collin,
born in Northeast, in Dutchess county, N. Y., April 23d,
1794, and married Anna Smith, of Dutchess, county,
January 2d, 1817, by whom he has had seven children :

    Edmund, born December 28th, 1817; died December
        29th, 1817.
    Caroline, born December 26th, 1818.
    Lucy B., born March 15th, 1821.

David, born August 23d, 1822.
Harriette, born November 15th, 1824.
Miriam, born May 16th, 1828.
Anna Smith, born October 4th, 1829.

CAROLINE COLLIN, daughter of David and Anna Smith Collin, born at Fayetteville, N. Y., December 26th, 1818, and married Sylvester Gardner, of Manlius, N. Y., September, 25th, 1838, by whom she has had seven children :

Edmund, born June 20th, 1840 ; died June 21st, 1840.
Caroline, born January 16th, 1842.
Sylvester, born November 18th, 1844.
Sarah, born January 21st, 1849.
Anna, born December 11th, 1850.
Miriam, born September 6th, 1852.
William, born March 26th, 1861.

LUCY B. COLLIN, daughter of David and Anna Smith Collin, born at Fayetteville, N. Y., March 15th, 1821, and married Porter Tremain, September 28th, 1841, by whom she has had two children :

Charles, born April 23d, 1843.
Porter, born January 24th, 1845.

DAVID COLLIN, son of David and Anna Smith Collin, born at Fayetteville, N. Y., August 23d, 1822, and married Clara Park, of Burlington, Otsego county, N. Y., October 22d, 1845, by whom he has had nine children :

David, born January 6th, 1847 ; died November 3d, 1862.
Edward, born September 30th, 1848.
Clara Park, born May 25th, 1850.
Roswell Park, born January 4th, 1852.

Charles Lee, born November 23d, 1853.

Harriette, born August 14th, 1856.

Miriam, born February 7th, 1859.

William Taylor, born March 28th, 1861.

David Francis, born November 16th, 1863.

HARRIETTE COLLIN, daughter of David and Anna Smith Collin, born at Fayetteville, N. Y., November 15th, 1824, and married Nathan Seward, of New Hartford, N. Y., June 13th, 1848 ; died at Fayetteville, February 17th, 1855. Her children were :

Harriette, born March 19th, 1849.

Anna, born May 26th, 1850.

Nathan, born November 24th, 1851; died November 28th, 1851.

Lucy, born July 17th, 1853.

Elizabeth, born February 13th, 1855 ; died April 18th, 1855.

MIRIAM COLLIN, daughter of David and Anna Smith Collin, born at Fayetteville, N. Y., May 16th, 1828, and married Ethan Armstrong, of Bennington, Vermont, May 15th, 1851, by whom she has had four children :

Geneva, born March 5th, 1852.

David, born June 11th, 1853.

Ethan Hamilton, born March 19th, 1836 ; died June 12th, 1862.

Augustus Tremain, born October 18th, 1863.

ANNA SMITH COLLIN, daughter of David and Anna Smith Collin, born at Fayetteville, N. Y., October 4th, 1829, and married Samuel James Wells, of New Hartford, N. Y., October 12th, 1854, by whom she has had four children :

Samuel James, born September 5th, 1856.
David Collin, born September 23rd, 1858.
John Lewis, born December 26th, 1860.
Paul Irving, born March 9th, 1863.

LUCY COLLIN, daughter of David and Lucy Bingham Collin, born at Hillsdale, June 27th, 1796, and married Barnet Wager, of Hillsdale, January 7th, 1815.

HARRIET COLLIN, daughter of David and Lucy Bingham Collin, born at Hillsdale, February 9th, 1799, and married Frederick Mesick of Claverack, March 3d, 1823; died February 28th, 1826.

LEE COLLIN, son of David and Lucy Bingham Collin, born at Hillsdale, February 14th, 1801, and married Almira Loop, daughter of the Hon. Henry Loop, of Hillsdale, November 19th, 1824, and upon her decease he married Lydia Smith, of Amenia, N. Y., September 1st, 1829; died at Hannibal, N. Y., May 4th, 1832.

HANNAH COLLIN, daughter of David and Lucy Bingham Collin, born in Hillsdale, October 2d, 1803, and married to David L. Farnham of Benson, Vermont, June 12th, 1829, by whom she had three children:

> Samuel, born December 28th, 1835; died January 11th, 1836.
> Rosamond D., born July 9th 1837.
> Almina, born September 23d, 1839.

Mrs. Hannah Collin Farnham died May 17th, 1863.

SOLOMON BINGHAM COLLIN, son of David and Lucy Bingham Collin, born at Hillsdale, March 7th, 1806, and married to Julia Ann Bushnell, daughter of John and Loxey

Lay Bushnell, of Hillsdale, October 13th, 1835, by whom he has had eight children :

Martha, born December 5th, 1836.

James Lee, born July 1st, 1838.

John Bingham, born April 4th, 1840.

Julia Ann, born July 16th, 1843.

Mary Louise, born July 21st, 1846.

Abby, born April 26th, 1850; died April 5th, 1854.

Lois Ann, born February 12th, 1853.

Viola, born May 26th. 1855; died March 17th, 1871.

AMANDA COLLIN, daughter of David and Lucy Bingham Collin, born at Hillsdale, February 18th, 1809, and married Porter Tremain, of Hillsdale, November 11th, 1830; died at Fayetteville, N. Y., March 26th, 1840. She had one son—Augustus, born March 27th, 1834.

NORTON SMITH COLLIN, son of David and Lucy Bingham Collin, born at Hillsdale, February 24th, 1812, and married to Eliza Park, of Burlington, Otsego county, N. Y., September 23d, 1837, by whom he has had five children :

Eliza, born February 27th, 1839.

Lucy, born February 21st, 1841.

Norton Park, born June 9th, 1842.

Virginia, born August 26th, 1851; died August 21st, 1856.

Cardora, born May 10th, 1858.

He represented the Second Assembly District of Columbia county in the State Legislature in 1861, and now resides in Brooklyn, N. Y.

ELIZA COLLIN, daughter of Norton S. and Eliza Park Collin, born in Hillsdale, February 27th, 1839, and married Rev. Lorenzo M. Gates, September 23d, 1862; died in Ottowa, La Salle county, Illinois, July 9th, 1869.

LUCY COLLIN, daughter of Norton S. and Eliza Park Collin, born in Hillsdale, February 21st, 1841, and married John Bingham Collin, son of Solomon Bingham and Julia Ann Bushnell Collin, of Hillsdale, August 11th, 1864, and now resides in the city of New York.

NORTON PARK COLLIN, son of Norton S. and Eliza Park Collin, born in Hillsdale, June 9th, 1842, and married Abby Greenwood, of Northampton, Mass., June, 1867, by whom he has one child, Edith Park, born June 15th, 1868. He now resides in Brooklyn, N. Y.

MARTHA COLLIN, daughter of Solomon Bingham and Julia Ann Bushnell Collin, born in Hillsdale, December 5th, 1836, and married Rev. Quincy J. Collin, son of John F. and Pamelia Jane Tullar Collin, March 28th, 1860, by whom she has had three children:

Carrie Louise, born January 14th, 1862.

May Amelia, born May 15th, 1865 ; died March 18th, 1869.

Grace Adelia, born July 19th, 1868.

JAMES LEE COLLIN, son of Solomon Bingham and Julia Ann Bushnell Collin, born in Hillsdale, July 1st, 1838, and married to Susan Culver, of Syracuse, N. Y., where he now resides.

JOHN BINGHAM COLLIN, son of Solomon Bingham and Julia Ann Bushnell Collin, born in Hillsdale, April 4th, 1840, and married Lucy Collin, daughter of Norton S. and Eliza Park Collin, of Brooklyn, N. Y., August 11th, 1864, and now resides in the city of New York. He was a captain of a company in the 91st Regiment of New York Volunteers during most of the late civil war.

HANNAH COLLIN, daughter of David and Lucy Smith Collin, born in Dutchess county, 1765, and married Squire

Sherwood and settled in Hillsdale, where she died at an advanced age, having had five children: Esther, Hannah; Sally, born 1787; Lucy, born 1788, and Susan, born June 4th, 1795; died June 11th, 1869.

LUCY COLLIN, daughter of David and Esther Gillett Collin, born in Dutchess county, N. Y., February 28th, 1773, and married Elijah Burton, January 3d, 1796. Died June 30th, 1847. She has had eleven children :

Collin, born December 29th, 1797.

Ely, born October 10th, 1799 ; died February 23d, 1860.

Belinda, born July 23d, 1801; died August 20th, 1864.

Lucinda, born December 1st, 1802 ; died January 21st, 1863.

Harriet, born January 28th, 1805.

Henry, born March 18th, 1807.

Miranda, born April 10th, 1809.

Benson, born July 17th, 1811 ; died August 25th, 1862.

David, born August 23d, 1813 ; died October 14th, 1813.

George Trafford, born August 10th, 1814.

Julia A., born June 21st, 1817.

SALLY COLLIN, daughter of David and Esther Gillett Collin, born in Dutchess county, N. Y., 1775, and married Douglass Clark, and settled in North East, Dutchess county, N. Y. They have had six children :

Perry, who married Caroline Winchell.

Henry, who married Betsey Ann Wheeler.

Olive.

Sally, who married Alexander Trowbridge.

Caroline, who married Caleb D. Barrett.

Emeline, who married Hampton Wheeler.

JAMES COLLIN, son of David and Esther Gillett Collin, born in Dutchess county, N. Y., April 15th, 1777, and married Lydia Hamblin, April 21st, 1804 ; died July 15th, 1856. His children were :

Eli, born February 23d, 1805.
James Hamblin, born March 5th, 1808.
Lydia Louise, born June 15th 1810.
Julia Ann, born November 17th, 1813.
Caroline, born September 21st, 1817.
Cordelia, born April 6th, 1820.
Aulia, born April 6th, 1820 ; died April 6th, 1820.
David Nelson, born March 17th, 1823 ; died March 3d, 1840.

ELI COLLIN, son of James and Lydia Hamlin Collin, born February 23d, 1805, and married Betsey Finch, February 12th, 1830 ; died June 12th, 1861.

JAMES HAMBLIN COLLIN, son of James and Lydia Hamblin Collin, born March 5th, 1808, and married Louise Wheeler, September 11th, 1845 ; died January 27th, 1860.

LYDIA LOUISE COLLIN, daughter of James and Lydia Hamblin Collin, born September 21st, 1817, and married Charles Mead April 3d, 1840.

CORDELIA COLLIN, daughter of James and Lydia Hamblin Collin, born April 6th, 1820, and married Barak Wilson, September, 1840 ; died February, 1845.

CHARLES PRENTICE ADAMS, son of Dr. L. S. Adams, born in Stockbridge, Mass., and married to Margaret Gavit, daughter of John E. and Margaret Sophia Robinson Gavit, October 8th, 1868.

JOHN ADAMS, second President of the United States, born at Braintree, Mass., October 19th, 1735, graduated at the Harvard University, 1755, and married Abigail Smith, daughter of Rev. William Smith, of Weymouth, and granddaughter of John Quincy, of Boston, in 1764; died July 4th, 1826. Among his children was John Quincy Adams, sixth President of the United States, who was born July 11th, 1767, just two days before the death of his distinguished great grandfather, John Quincy, and whose paternal estate he subsequently inherited.

ETHAN ARMSTRONG, born in Bennington, Vermont, April 24th, 1810, and married Miriam Collin, daughter of David and Anna Smith Collin, May 15th, 1851, by who he has had four children:

Geneva, born March 5th, 1852.
David, born June 11, 1853.
Ethan Hamilton, born March 19th, 1856; died June 12th, 1862.
Augustus Tremain, born October 18th, 1863.

ANTHONY ARNOLD, born in Dutchess county, N. Y., April 12th, 1704, and married Sarah ————, who was born 1712. They were Friend Quakers, and had two children:

David, born May 27th, 1733.
Sarah, born May 24th, 1742.

DAVID ARNOLD, son of Anthony and Sarah Arnold, born in Dutchess county, N. Y., May 27th, 1733, and died in Gorham, Ontario county, N. Y., at a very advanced age. His wife, Hannah, was born in Dutchess county, May 3d, 1736, by whom he had seven children:

Mary, born May 24th, 1758.
Phebe, born May 31st, 1760.
George, born August 9th, 1762.

Anthony, born December 1st, 1766.
Jonathan, born March 1st, 1771.
Sarah, born May 5th, 1773.
David, born January 1st, 1776.

SARAH ARNOLD, daughter of Anthony and Sarah Arnold, born May 24th, 1742, and married John Collin, son of John and Hannah Merwin Collin, of Milford, Conn., September 16th, 1758, died at Hillsdale, N. Y., December 29th, 1791. Her children were :

Anthony, born February 24th, 1760.
Hannah, born June 7th, 1763.
John, born September 19th, 1772.

MARY ARNOLD, daughter of David and Hannah Arnold, born May 24th, 1758, and married to John Wager, of Hillsdale, N. Y. They had one son :
Barnet, born January 29th, 1793.

SARAH ARNOLD, daughter of David and Hannah Arnold, born May 5th, 1773, and married Ezekiel Whalen, of Milton, Saratoga county, N. Y., by whom she had several children, one of whom was named Seth.

CHARLES ATWATER, born in New Haven, Conn., August 18th, 1786, and married to Mary Merwin, daughter of Miles and Abigail Beach Merwin, of Milford, Conn., October, 1809; died February 21st, 1825. His children were :

George Merwin, born October 29th, 1814, now a resident of Springfield, Mass.
David P. Atwater, M. D., residing in Bridgeport, Conn.
James C. Atwater, residing in Brooklyn, N. Y.

His father, Jeremiah Atwater, was born in Wallingford, Conn., November 10th, 1744.
His grandfather, John Atwater, born in December, 1718.

His great grandfather, John Atwater, born in Wallingford, Conn., August 17th, 1683.

His great-great grandfather, David Atwater, born in New Haven, November 1st, 1654, and was one of the first planters of New Haven county, and in the first division of land among the settlers a farm was assigned him in the Neck, as the tract was called, between Mill'and Quinnipiach rivers. Upon that tract he lived until his death, which occurred October 5th, 1692. Rev. Charles Atwater was a devoted minister of the gospel, having graduated at Yale College in 1805.

TRYPENA BLANSET, born in Jerusalem, Yates county, N. Y., January 10th, 1836, and married to Charles Willis Bartholomew, son of John Moss and Tabitha Paulina Tullar Bartholomew, February 26th, 1863. Her children are :

Edward Willis, born June 7th, 1864.
Wilson Thomas, born April 28th, 1869.
Arthur Dana, born April 5th, 1871.

JOHN MOSS BARTHOLOMEW, born in Wallingford, Conn., February 22d, 1800, and married Tabitha Paulina Tullar, daughter of Charles and Rebecca Race Tullar, of Egremont, Mass., October 8th, 1822, by whom he has had two children :

Charles Willis, born September 14th, 1825.
Pamelia Jane, born December 28th, 1827.

CHARLES WILLIS BARTHOLOMEW, son of John Moss and Tabitha Paulina Tullar Bartholomew, born in Sheffield, Mass., September 14th, 1825, and married Tryphina Blanset, February 26th, 1863, by whom he has had three sons :

Edward Willis, born June 7th, 1864.
Wilson Thomas, born April 28th, 1869.
Arthur Dana, born April 5th, 1871.

PAMELIA JANE BARTHOLOMEW, daughter of John Moss and Tabitha Paulina Tullar Bartholomew, born in Sheffield, Mass., December 28th, 1827, and married to Henry Stiles Barbour, of Canton, Conn., November 25th, 1851, and now resides in Hartford, Conn. Her children are :

John Humphry, born May 29th, 1854.
Edward Willis, born May 2d, 1857; died May 28th, 1861.
Lucy Amelia, born May 6th, 1863.

HENRY STILES BARBOUR, born in Canton, Conn., August 2d, 1822, and married Pamelia Jane Bartholomew, daughter of John Moss and Tabitha Paulina Tullar Bartholomew, Nov. 25th, 1851, by whom he has had three children, John Humphry, Edward Willis and Lucy Amelia. He was an attorney at law, and for about twenty years was a resident of Wolcottville, Litchfield county, Conn., and in 1871 moved to Hartford, Conn. He had been a member of the Connecticut Legislature, and in 1871 was a member of the State Senate, serving as chairman of the Judiciary Committee.

HENRY BARBOUR, of Canton, Conn., was married to Naoma Humphry, of Barkhamstead, Conn., April 2d, 1817. Their children were :

Clarinda, born April 17th, 1818.
Hernon Humphry, born July 19th, 1820.
Henry Stiles, born August 2d, 1822.
Lucy, born May 7th, 1824.
Pluma, born September 17th, 1826.
Juliette, born January 20th, 1828.
Sylvester, born January 20th, 1831.
Naoma Ellen, born February 3d, 1833.
Edward Payson, born September 23d, 1834.

SYLVESTER BARBOUR, son of Henry and Naoma Humphry Barbour, born at Canton, Conn., January 20th, 1831, and married Frances Amelia Collin, daughter of John Francis and Pamelia Jane Tullar Collin, of Hillsdale, N. Y., November 27th, 1860, and settled as an attorney at law in Ansonia, New Haven county, Conn. His children are :

Lizzie Lawrence, born September 21st, 1861.
Collin Henry, born July 6th, 1863.
Edward Humphry, born 1867; died February 13th, 1869.
Amy Louise, born September 25th, 1869.

LORING BARTLET, of New York, married Augusta Foster, daughter of Seymour and Sarah Madaline Truesdell Foster, and resides in New York city.

DELANEY BARTLET married Almira Farnham, daughter of David L. and Hannah Collin Farnham, January 3d, 1863.

RICHARD BARTLET, son of Richard Bartlet, of Boston, at which place he was born, married Mary Robinson, daughter of Gain and Margaret Watson Robinson, of East Bridgewater, Mass. The following were their children :

Lydia, born 1757 ; married John Savage.
Mary, born 1759 ; married Benjamin Richards.
Margaret, born 1761 ; married James Taylor.
Gain, born 1763 ; married —— McNeal.
Martha ——, married Andrew Mushero.
Richard.
Elizabeth.
Robert.
Edward.
Jane ——, married Shadrack Holley.
William.

JERUSHA BARTLET, daughter of Ebenezer Bartlet, of Duxbury, Mass., born 1731, and married James Robinson, of Bridgewater, Mass.; died March 24th, 1812. Her children were : James, Bartlet, Watson, Abner, Gain, Clark, Jerusha, Bartlet, Margaret, Mary, Elizabeth, Jane, Esther, Eleanor, Bethia and Martha.

PETER BECKER, born April 15th, 1759 ; married Mary Southard, and died June 21st, 1839. She died October 25th, 1837.

JOHN P. BECKER, son of Peter and Mary Southard Becker, born September 28th, 1782, and married Elizabeth Clum, December 2d, 1804 ; died December, 1859. She was born July 24th, 1782 ; died November 19th, 1847. Their children were :

Philip, born June 22d, 1805.

Polly, born April 9th, 1807.

David Lonson, born January 20th, 1809.

Stephen C., born August 4th, 1811.

Lovina, born May 8th, 1813.

Elizabeth, born December 3d, 1815.

Julianne, born May 22d, 1817.

Catharine, born August 18th, 1820.

Margaret Caroline, born October 28th, 1822.

MARGARET CAROLINE BECKER, daughter of John Pond, Elizabeth Clum Becker, born October 28th, 1822, and married Edward Duncan, March 8th, 1852, by whom she had two children :

Carrie Margaret, born June 6th, 1856.

Edward Jennings, born February 22d, 1854; died ——.

After the decease of Edward Duncan, on the 10th of October, 1862, she married Orrin M. Sawyer, of Austerlitz, September 4th, 1864.

Philip Becker, son of John P. and Elizabeth Clum Becker, born June 22d, 1805, and married Elizabeth DeGroff, July 22d, 1827. Their children are :

Henry L., born July 15th, 1828.

James M., born June 29th, 1831.

Luman F., born December 20th, 1833; died December 24th, 1866.

Jane, born April 16th, 1836.

Julia, born October 12th, 1837.

Emma H., born September 28th, 1840.

Philip, born December 19th, 1843.

Charlie, born April 28th, 1846.

Hiram H., born May 10th, 1848.

Mary, born December 20th, 1850; died September 6th, 1852.

Henry L. Becker, son of Philip and Elizabeth De Groff Becker, born July 15th, 1828, and married Jane A. Carskaden, November 17th, 1851. Their children were :

Eugene, born March 22d, 1854; died August 22d, 1856.

Altanah, born August 23d, 1852; died February 3d, 1863.

James M. Becker, son of Philip and Elizabeth De Groff Becker, born December 20th, 1833, and married Maria A. Clark, December 1st, 1861. Their children are :

James, born February 11th, 1864.

Charlie, born March, 1866.

Lilly, born April 15th, 1870.

Julia Becker, daughter of Philip and Elizabeth De Groff Becker, born October 12th, 1837, and married Andrew J. Kittell, of Hudson, April 28th, 1859; died July 9th, 1861. Their infant child died a few weeks after.

JANE BECKER, daughter of Philip and Elizabeth De Groff Becker, born April 16th, 1836, and married John F. Collin, son of John and Ruth Holman Johnson Collin, January 16th, 1871.

PHILIP BECKER, son of Philip and Elizabeth De Groff Becker, born December 19th, 1843, and married Cynthia Augusta Truesdell, July 15th, 1866. Their children are:

Julia Elizabeth, born April 26th, 1867.
Gordon, born September 9th, 1868.

DAVID LONSON BECKER, son of John P. and Elizabeth Clum Becker, born January 20th, 1809, and married Sarah Truesdell, daughter of Samuel Truesdell. After her decease, he married Ruth A. Tyler, daughter of John Tyler. After her decease, he married Mary Osborn, daughter of Melvin Osborn.

By his wife Sarah, he had two children, Alfred and Sarah.

By his wife Ruth, he had two children, Franklin and Lonson.

By his wife Mary, he has one child, Lizzie.

STEPHEN C. BECKER, son of John P. and Elizabeth Clum Becker, born August 4th, 1811, and married Eunice Krum. Their children were: Porter A., John, Mary A., Ellen, Alice, and Lonson J.

LOVINA BECKER, daughter of John P. and Elizabeth Clum Becker, born May 8th, 1813, and married Orville McAlpin, son of John McAlpin, January 1st, 1851. Their children were:

Mary C., born November 25th, 1851; died September 15th, 1855.
Lucy, born September 3d, 1857.

ELIZABETH BECKER, daughter of John P. and Elizabeth Clum Becker, born December 3d, 1815, and married Sylvanus Smith, and resides in Penn Yan, Yates county, N. Y.

JULIANNE BECKER, daughter of John P. and Elizabeth Clum Becker, born May 22d, 1817, and married Samuel Voak, by whom she has one son, Arthur. They now reside in Waukegan, Lake county, Illinois.

CATHARINE BECKER, daughter of John P. and Elizabeth Clum Becker, born August 18th, 1820, and married Peter J. Becker, son of Joseph and Betsy Smith Becker, November 14th, 1840. Their children were : George W., Gains T., Francis E., Lucy and Charles W.; the two last of whom have died.

POLLY BECKER, daughter of John P. and Elizabeth Clum Becker, born April 9th, 1807, and married Gains Truesdell, son of Samuel Truesdell, of Hillsdale. There children were : John, Ruth, Stephen, Elizabeth, Juliette.

EDWARD WELLS BLACKINGTON, of Adams, Mass., married Camille Eugenia Van Dusen, daughter of Freeman and Lucretia Tullar Van Dusen, October 1st, 1862, by whom he has had two children.

ISAAC J. BIGELOW was born in Leominster. Worcester county, Mass., February 24th, 1809, and graduated at the medical college at Cincinnati, Ohio, and married Hannah Matthew, widow of Zelotes Matthew, and sister of the Rev. Leonidas Lent Hamlin, December 1st, 1838.

JOHN BRADEN, born August 18th, 1826, and married Pamelia Laurania Collin, daughter of John Francis and Pamelia Jane Tullar Collin, October 16, 1856. Their children were :

Mary Eliza, born August 11th, 1858.

Francis Collin, born February 20th, 1860 : died July 20th, 1860.

Fannie, born June 23d, 1866 ; died September 18th, 1866.

He graduated at the university in Delaware, Ohio, then under the presidency of Edward Thompson, who subsequently became a bishop of the Methodist Episcopal Church. Having obtained a license to preach in the Methodist Episcopal Church, he joined the Cincinnati Conference, in which he labored for some years, and is now a member of the Tennessee Conference and is residing in Nashville.

JAMES BRADISH, born 1675, died 1763. His wife was born 1688, died 1769. They had one son, John, born 1719, who married Mary Green, who was born 1720 ; died 1784 ; and he died 1781. They had eight children :

Sarah, born 1774, and married Mr. Nye.
Hannah, born 1748.
John, born 1750.
James, born 1752 ; married Jane Townsend.
Mary, born 1754 ; married Mr. Green, of Hardwick, Mass.
Dinah, born 1757.
Ruth, born 1760, and married Mr. Palmer.
Joseph, born 1762.

JOHN BRADISH, son of John and Mary Green Bradish, born 1750, and married Hannah Warner, of Hardwick. Massachussetts, who was born 1752; died 1828, in Palmyra, N. Y.

He was a colonel in the militia, and held important offices in church and state, and died in Palmyra, N. Y., 1825. They had seven children :

Calvin, born in Hardwick, 1773; died in Michigan.
Chloe, born in Hardwick, 1775.
Charles, born in Hardwick, 1778.
Sarah, born in Cummington, Mass., 1781.
Luther, born in Cummington, 1783.
Calvin, 2d, born in Cummington.

CHLOE BRADISH, daughter of John and Hannah Warner Bradish, born in Hardwick, Mass., 1775, and married to Gain Robinson, son of James and Jerusha Bartlet Robinson, of Cummington, Mass., 1796. She died in Stockbridge, Mass., 1866. Her children were : Amanda, William Cullen, Cains Cassius, Abigail Blackman. Clark, Erasmus Darwin, Charles Rollin, Chloe, Hellen Elizabeth, and Margaret Sophia.

SARAH BRADISH, daughter of John and Hannah Warner Bradish, born in Cummington, 1781, and married Bartlet Robinson; died 1853.

CHARLES BRADISH, son of John and Hannah Warner Bradish, born in Hardwick, Mass., 1778, and died in Madison, Michigan, 1857. He married Bethia Robinson, daughter of James and Jerusha Bartlet Robinson, 1804, and moved from Cummington, Mass., to Palmyra, N. Y., in 1807. He was one of the New York electors at the election of President Harrison. His children were : Alexander H., William F., Seth W., Bartlet R., Lucretia E., and Philander.

LUTHER BRADISH, son of John and Hannah Warner Bradish, born in Cummington, Mass., 1783; died in New York, 1863. He was elected Lieut.-Governor of the State of New York in November, 1838. With a splendid person and high moral character, he possessed superior talents.

Rowena Bradish, daughter of John and Hannah Warner Bradish, born 1786, and married John Comstock, 1801, and settled in the town of Rasin, Michigan. Her husband died, 1851. She had ten children : Worrener M., Walter R., Francis A., Hannah W., Luther B., Calvin B., Mary S., Charles B., Lauriston A., and Addis E.

Calvin Bradish, son of John and Hannah Warner Bradish, born in Cummington, Mass., and married Nancy Post, of Long Island, N. Y., and had twelve children : Martha M., Curran, Nelson, Sarah, Luther, Calvin, John W., Hannah W., Augustus W., Amanda G., Myron H., and Norman F. He settled in Lenox county, Michigan, and bought a large tract of land, which he divided among his children. He died in 1854. His wife died in 1839.

Martha M. Bradish, daughter of Calvin and Nancy Post Bradish, born in Michigan, and married Norman B. Carter, and settled in Black Creek, Michigan. They had four children : Russell C., Amanda D., Francis N., and Nancy B.

Curran Bradish, son of Calvin and Nancy Post Bradish, born in Michigan, and married Roby Cumstock, and settled in Adrian, Michigan. Their children are : Hellen E., Thomas A., and Darius C.

Nelson Bradish, son of Calvin and Nancy Post Bradish, born in Michigan, and married Phebe Wilson, 1828, and settled in Adrian, Michigan. Their children are : Myron W., William C., Ann E., Warren C., Louisa, and Mary C.

Sarah Bradish, daughter of Calvin and Nancy Post Bradish, born in Michigan, and married Paul Jagger, 1827, and settled in East Palmyra, N. Y. Their children are : Luther B., Lucy A., and Charles E.

LUTHER BRADISH, son of Calvin and Nancy Post Bradish, born in Michigan, and married Rachael Moon, June, 1846.

CALVIN BRADISH, son of Calvin and Nancy Post Bradish, born in Michigan, and married Mary Ann Jennings, 1838, and settled in Lenawee county, Michigan. Their children are : Horace C., Orrin H., and Chloe C.

JOHN W. BRADISH, son of Calvin and Nancy Post Bradish, born in Michigan, and married Lydia A. Jeroleman, 1840, and settled in Lenawee county, Michigan. Their children are : Elizabeth F., Mary A., Sarah J., and Martha M.

HANNAH W. BRADISH, daughter of Calvin and Nancy Post Bradish, born in Michigan.

AUGUSTUS W. BRADISH, son of Calvin and Nancy Post Bradish, born in Michigan, and married Eliza M. Appleby, 1847, and settled in Lenawee county. Michigan. Their children are : Clarence M., Herbert H., and others.

AMANDA G. BRADISH, daughter of Calvin and Nancy Post Bradish, born in Michigan, and married Melvin T. Nickerman. 1844, and settled in Adrian, Michigan. Their children are : Calvin B., Norman F., Therese E., and Francis A.

MYRON H. BRADISH, son of Calvin and Nancy Post Bradish, born in Michigan, and drowned in the ninth year of his age.

NORMAN F. BRADISH, son of Calvin and Nancy Post Bradish, born in Michigan, and married Caroline M. Caton in 1845, and settled in Lenawee county, Michigan. Their children are : Mintha A., Hellen A., and Norman R.

ALEXANDER H. BRADISH, son of Calvin and Nancy Post Bradish, born in Michigan, and died in early childhood.

WILLIAM F. BRADISH, son of Charles and Bethia Robinson Bradish, born in Palmyra, N. Y., and married Rachael F. Warren in 1834, and settled in Medina, Michigan, in 1853. His wife died in 1862, and he married Perris De Forrest. His children are : Emma J., Chloe E., Clark R., and James Q.; the last of whom perished by the blowing up of a steamer on the Mississippi river while serving as a soldier in the late civil war.

CHARLES H. BRADISH, son of Charles and Bethia Robinson Bradish, born in Palmyra, N. Y., and married Amy Ann Aldrich in 1849, and in 1853, moved to Lenawee county, Michigan. His children are : Zimrhoda J., and Alexander H.

SETH W. BRADISH, son of Charles and Bethia Bradish, born in Palmyra, N. Y.; died in Michigan in 1837.

BARTLET R. BRADISH, son of Charles and Bethia Robinson Bradish, born in Palmyra, N. Y., and married Cora M. Philips, in 1857 ; died in Adrian, Michigan, in 1863.

LUCRETIA E. BRADISH, daughter of Charles and Bethia Robinson Bradish, born in Palmyra, N. Y., where she now resides. She has given some valuable assistance in this compilation.

PHILANDER P. BRADISH, son of Charles and Bethia Robinson Bradish, born in Palmyra, N. Y., and married Maria T. Bradley, of Lyons, in 1848, and settled in Batavia, N. Y. Their children are : John H., Edward F., William B., and Francis.

ELIJAH BURTON, born in Dutchess county, N. Y., July 31st, 1769, and married Lucy Collin, daughter of David and Esther Gillett Collin January 3d, 1796. Their children were :

Collin, born December 29th, 1797.

Ely, born October 30th, 1799; died February 23d, 1860.

Belinda, born July 23d, 1801; died August 20th, 1864.

Lucinda, born December 1st, 1802; died January 21st, 1863.

Harriet, born January 28th, 1805.

Henry, born March 18th, 1807.

Miranda, born April 10th, 1809.

Benson, born July 17th, 1811; died August 25th, 1862.

David, born August 23d, 1813; died October 14th, 1813.

George Trafford, born August 10th, 1814.

Julia A., born June 21st, 1817.

Elijah Burton, died February 7th, 1856.

HARRIET BURTON, daughter of Elijah and Lucy Collin Burton, born in Hillsdale, N. Y., January 28th, 1805, and married to Joshua Dakin, of Dutchess county. Their children are : Jane, Ambrose L., Jennett, Mariett, Chester E.

HENRY BURTON, son of Elijah and Lucy Collin Burton, born in Hillsdale, March 18th, 1807, and married Eliza Doan, October 29th, 1834. Their children are :

Sterling, born October 20th, 1836.

Lucy, born November 30th, 1838; died August 3d, 1857.

Henry Collin, born July 11th, 1843; died August 24th, 1848.

STERLING BURTON, son of Henry and Eliza Doan Burton, born in Hillsdale, October 20th, 1836, and married Martha L. Whiting, July 13th, 1864. Their children are :

Henry Collin, born August 22d, 1865.

Charles Whiting, born January 29th, 1868; died February 1st, 1868.

MIRANDA BURTON, daughter of Elijah and Lucy Collin Burton, born April 10th, 1809, and married George W. Bushnell, son of William Bushnell, of Hillsdale. Their children are : Mary Jane ; Josephine, died —— ; William Henry.

GEORGE TRAFFORD BURTON, son of Elijah and Lucy Collin Burton, born August 10th, 1814, and married Maria Everts, of Hillsdale. They have had one daughter, Urvilla.

JOHN BUSHNELL, son of George Bushnell, born in Hillsdale, September 26th, 1789, and married to Loxey Lay, of Saybrook, Conn., September 20th, 1810; died June 30th, 1842. Their children were :

Julia Ann, born September 18th, 1811.
Chloe, born January 1st, 1813.
Caroline, born October 21st, 1814.
George, born July 10th, 1816.
Elisha W., born December 27th, 1818.
John and Loxy, twins, born January 5th, 1821.
Lay, born February 28th, 1826.
Abby, born April 17th, 1828.
Ely, born April 3d, 1830.

JULIA ANN BUSHNELL, daughter of John and Loxey Lay Bushnell, born in Hillsdale, September 28th, 1811, and married to Solomon B. Collin, son of David and Lucy Bingham Collin, October 13th, 1835; died December 6th, 1865. Their children are :

Martha, born December 5th, 1836.
James Lee, born July 1st, 1838.

John Bingham, born April 4th, 1840.
Julia Ann, born July 16th, 1843.
Mary Louise, born July 21st, 1846.
Abby, born April 25th, 1850; died April 5th, 1854.
Lois Ann, born February 12th, 1853.
Viola, born May 26th, 1855; died March 17th, 1871.

CHLOE BUSHNELL, daughter of John and Loxey Lay Bushnell, born in Hillsdale, January 1st, 1813, and married to Arnold Fletcher Truesdell, son of Harvey and Clynthia Johnson Truesdell. Her children are: Morania, Julia, Emma, and Madeline.

ELISHA W. BUSHNELL, son of John and Loxey Lay Bushnell, born in Hillsdale, December 27th, 1818, and married to Emma House, daughter of Benjamin and Phebe Vanderburgh House, September 1st, 1840, by whom he had five children:

Sarah, born November 7th, 1841, and married Arthur Park, November, 20th, 1861.
George, born August 14th, 1843; died March 7th, 1845.
Mary Vanderburgh, born April 20th, 1847; died May 3d, 1848.
George Vanderburgh, born September 11th, 1851.
Clayton, born October 23d, 1857; died November 21st, 1859.

His wife, Emma House Bushnell, died November 16th, 1859, and on the 12th day of February, 1862, he married Frances L. Orton, who died August 1st, 1865, and on the 25th of April he married Catharine Martin Roe.

GEORGE W. BUSHNELL, son of William Bushnell, born in Hillsdale, and married Miranda Burton, daughter of Elijah and Lucy Collin Burton, and now resides in the

State of Illinois. His children were: Mary Jane; Josephine, died; William Henry.

JOHN CARY, born in Somersetshire, England, emigrated to this country in 1639, and settled in Duxbury, Mass., and married Elizabeth, daughter of Francis Godfrey, 1644. He subsequently became an original proprietor, and among the first settlers, of West Bridgwater, Mass., and was the first town clerk. He died in 1681, and his wife died in 1680. Their children were:

John, born at Duxbury, 1645.
Francis, born at Duxbury, 1647.
Elizabeth, born at Duxbury, 1649.
James, born at Braintree, 1652.
Mary, born at Bridgwater, 1654.
Jonathan, born at Bridgwater, 1656.
David, born at Bridgwater, 1658.
Hannah, born at Bridgwater, 1661.
Joseph, born at Bridgwater, 1663.
Rebecca, born at Bridgwater, 1665.
Sarah, born at Bridgwater, 1667.
Mehitabel, born at Bridgwater, 1670.

EZRA CARY, the grandson of Francis Cary, and great grandson of John and Elizabeth Godfrey Cary, married Mary, daughter of Col. John Holman, and great aunt of Ruth Holman Collin, in 1737. He settled in New Jersey, and had two children: Sarah, born 1738, and Shepherd, born 1742.

EPHRAIM CARY, great grandson of John Cary, married Jane, daughter of Capt. John Holman, 1771. Their children were: Salome, born 1774; Jane, 1773; Cyrus, 1777; William Holman, 1779; Ephraim, 1782; Shepherd, 1784; Susanna, 1787; Francis, 1789; Jason, 1791; Adenith, 1793;

Harmony, 1796. His wife, Jane, died, 1809, and he died, 1828.

JOSEPH CARY, son of John and Elizabeth Godfrey Cary, was born in Bridgewater, Mass., 1663, and moved to Windham, Conn., and is the ancestor of the distinguished writers of poetry, Phebe and Alice Cary, and also of Gen. S. F. Cary, of College Hill, Ohio.

The ancestors of John Cary were Norman French, one of whom was an officer in the army of William the Conqueror, who cantoned out the country to his men, and Mr. Cary thereby became an extensive land owner in Sommersetshire. In the subsequent civil wars the owner of the Cary property took sides in behalf of Richard Second, against Henry Fourth, and the property, in consequence, became confiscated to the Crown. In the beginning of the reign of Henry Fifth, an Arragonian Knight, after having passed triumphantly through divers countries, went to England and challenged any man of his rank and quality to make trial of his valor in arms. Sir Robert Cary accepted the challenge, and the combat was waged in Smithfield, London. The contest was long and doubtful, but finally terminated in favor of Sir Robert Cary, and the king, in consequence, restored to him a large part of the confiscated lands and authorized him to bear the coat of arms of the Knights of Arragon. Gen. S. F. Cary has supplied me with a pictorial representation of that coat of arms, and he and Miss Phebe Cary have kindly given me much valuable information in respect to their kindred.

DOUGLASS CLARK, of Dutchess county, N. Y., married Sally Collin, daughter of David and Esther Gillett Collin, and settled in the town of North East. Their children are :

Perry, who married Caroline Winchell.
Henry, who married Betsey Ann Wheeler.
Olive.
Sally, who married Alexander Trowbridge.
Caroline, who married Caleb D. Barrett.
Emmeline, who married Hampton Wheeler.

AMBROSE CLARK, of Dutchess county, N. Y., married
Julia Ann Collin, daughter of James and Lydia Hamblin
Collin. Their children are:

Edward, born July 6th, 1835; died July 30th, 1835.
Julia Ann, born May 7th, 1840.
Ambrose, born September 17th, 1842.
James M. born December 12th, 1844.
Howard, born September 24th, 1849; died, March,
1850.
Hattie L., born January 13th, 1852.
Seward, born December 24th, 1854; died January 2d,
1867.

ALICE CARY, a descendant of John Cary, one of the
original proprietors of Bridgewater, Mass., was born in
Cincinnati, Ohio, 1822; died in New York, February,
2d, 1871, while in poetic talent she ranked high among her
contemporaries. She was equally distinguished for her
social qualifications.

PHEBE CARY, a daughter of John Cary, of Bridgewater,
Mass., and sister of Alice Cary, and niece of Gen. S. F.
Cary, of College Hill, Ohio, was born in Cincinnati, Ohio,
in 1825; died in Newport, Rhode Island, August 1st, 1871.
Like her sister, she was social, amiable and respected by
all, and the following birth-day tribute to her friend, Miss
Susan B. Anthony, indicates the good-natured poetic talent
with which she was endowed:

4

We touch our caps, and place to-night
   The victor's wreath upon her,
The woman who outranks us all
   In courage and in honor.

While others in domestic broils,
   Have proved by word and carriage,
That one of the United States
   Is not the state of marriage.

The caring not the loss of men,
   Nor for the world's confusion,
Has carried on a civil war
   And made a revolution.

True, other women have been brave
   When banded or husbanded;
But she has bravely fought her way
   Alone and single handed.

And think of her unselfish strength,
   Her generous disposition,
Who never made a lasting prop
   Out of a proposition.

She might have chosen an honored name,
   And none have scorned or hissed it;
Have written Mrs. Jones or Smith,
   But strange to say she missed it.

For fifty years to come may she
   Grow rich and ripe and mellow,
Be quoted even above par,
   Or any other fellow.

And speak the truth from pole to pole,
   And keep her light a-burning,
Before she cuts her stick to go
   The way there's no returning.

Because her motto grand has been,
   The right of every human;
And first and last, and right or wrong,
   She takes the side of woman.

A perfect woman, nobly planned,
To aid, not to amuse one;
Take her for all and all, we ne'er
Shall see the match for Susan.

ISAAC COON, born May 22d, 1824, and married Elmira Becker, daughter of John P. and Elizabeth Ann Becker, September 28th, 1850. Their childern are :

Edwin Allworth, born October 13th, 1863.
John Henry, born September 22d, 1855.
Eugene Smith, born July 5th, 1864.
Orrin M., born October 4th, 1865.
Sidney N., born February 18th, 1869.

Mr. CORBETT, of Plymouth, Mass., married Betty, daughter of Gain and Margaret Watson Robinson, and had one daughter, Betsey.

BETSEY CORBETT, daughter of Mr. and Betty Robinson Corbett, born in Cummington, Mass., and married David Orr, of Hillsdale, N. Y. ; and upon the death of David Orr, she married John Van Dusen, of Hillsdale.

LORENZO L. CROWNS, of Washington, D. C., married Mary Collin, daughter of James and Velona Hill Collin, December 27th, 1859, by whom he has two sons.

LUCRETIA E. CHURCH, born May 1st, 1825, and married Charles A. Tullar, son of Seneca C. and Mary A. Gordon Tullar, November 10th, 1844.

SILAS L. CHURCH, born September 22d, 1820, and married Pamelia Jane Tullar, daughter of Seneca C. and Mary A. Gordon Tullar, December 26th, 1851. Their children are :

Minnesota, born April 19th, 1853.
Virginia, born June 17th, 1859.

ELIZABETH CHURCH, born July 24th, 1823, and married William Frederick Tullar, son of Charles and Rebecca Race Tullar, November 25th, 1841; died July 6th, 1842.

OLIVER DAVIDSON, of Canterbury, Conn., born 1754, and married to Deidama Morse, 1779; died 1787. Their children were :

Oliver, born in Canterbury, 1781.
Joseph, born in Canterbury, 1783.
Anna, born in Canterbury, 1785.

OLIVER DAVIDSON, son of Oliver and Deidama Morse Davidson, born in Canterbury, Conn., 1781, and married to Mary Miller, of Dutchess county, N. Y. They had several children, among whom was Lucretia Maria and Margaret Miller Davidson, who, though dying at an early age, had poetic talent which has procured their names places in Appleton's Cyclopedia of Biography, and Drake's Dictionary of American Biography. He was a physician, and died in Plattsburgh, N. Y.

JOSEPH DAVIDSON, son of Oliver and Deidama Morse Davidson, born in Canterbury, Conn, 1783, and married and had several children ; but he and all his children are dead, except one son, Erastus, who resides in Lansingburgh, N. Y.

ANNA DAVIDSON, daughter of Oliver and Deidama Morse Davidson, born in Canterbury, Conn., 1785, and married to Aaron Ford, of Hillsdale, N. Y. ; died May 5th, 1839. She had no children.

LUCRETIA MARIA DAVIDSON, daughter of Oliver and Mary Miller Davidson, and granddaughter of Deidama Morse Collin, born in Plattsburgh, N. Y., September 27th, 1808; died August 27th, 1825. In October, 1824, a gentleman who knew her intense desire for education, placed her at a female seminary in Troy, N. Y., where her incessant application soon destroyed her constitution, previously debilitated by disease, and she died before completing her 17th year. A biographical sketch, with a collection of her poems, was published by S. F. B. Morse, in 1829, entitled "Amir Khan, and other poems," the remains of L. M. Davidson. Although a great part of her compositions were destroyed, 278 remain. Her biography has been written by Catharine M. Sedgwick, in 1843.

MARGARET MILLER DAVIDSON, sister of Lucretia Maria Davidson and granddaughter of Deidama Morse Collin, born March 26th, 1823; died November 25th, 1837. Sharing her sister's precocity, she began to write at six years of age. At ten she wrote and acted in a passionate drama in society, New York, and, notwithstanding the warning of her sister's fate, her intellectual activity was not restrained. Margaret's poems were issued under the auspices of Washington Irving, and the works of both sisters were published together, in 1850. A volume of selections from the writings of Miss Margaret M. Davidson, with a preface by Miss C. M. Sedgwick, appeared in 1843. Lieutenant L. P. Davidson, U. S. A., the brother of Margaret and Lucretia, who also died young, wrote verses with elegance and ease.

ROSWELL DERBYSHIRE, of Lenox, Mass., married Ellen H. Collin, daughter of James and Velona Hill Collin, May 9th, 1849; died on the Isthmus of Darien.

SPENCER EMOND, son of Isaiah Emond, of Hillsdale, married Sally Sherwood, daughter of Squire and Hannah Collin Sherwood.

ANNA ESMOND, daughter of Isaiah Esmond, was born in Hillsdale, and married John W. Truesdell, son of Thomas and Hannah Collin Truesdell, July 25th, 1804. Her children were :

Beebe, born June 5th, 1805 ; died April, 1811.
John W., born November 13th, 1806.

After the death of her husband, she married Refine Latting, by whom she had one daughter, Henrietta, who married Owen Bixby.

Mrs. Anna Latting died in 1870.

ELIZA ESMOND, daughter of Spencer and Sally Sherwood Esmond and granddaughter of Squire and Hannah Collin Sherwood, was born in Hillsdale, June 31st, 1816, and married Edward B. Hunt, son of Samuel and Sally Bagley Hunt, September 19th, 1866.

MARIA EVERTS, daughter of Henry Everts, born in Hillsdale, and married George Trafford Burton, son of Elijah and Lucy Collin Burton, by whom she has had a daughter, Urvilla.

DAVID L. FARNHAM, of Benson, Vermont, married Hannah Collin, daughter of David and Lucy Bingham Collin, June 12th, 1829 ; died January 17th, 1860. His children were :

Samuel, born December 23d, 1835 ; died July 11th, 1836.
Rosamond D., born July 9th, 1837.
Almina, born September 23d, 1839, and married Delaney Bartlet, January 8th, 1863.

ANDREW FORD, born in Abington, Mass., and married Maria Beal. They had eight children, viz. : Elias, Levi, Eleazar, Andrew, Sarah, Elizabeth, Matilda, and Jerusha. He was at the battle of Bunker Hill.

Levi Ford, son of Andrew and Maria Beal Ford, born in Cummington, Mass., and married Desire Whitman, of Chesterfield, Mass.

Ebenezer Ford, son of Andrew and Maria Beal Ford, born in Cummington, Mass., and married Huldah Otis, of Goshen, Mass.

Andrew Ford, son of Andrew and Maria Beal Ford, born in Cummington, and married Olive Baker, of Hawley, Mass.

Sarah Ford, daughter of Andrew and Maria Beal Ford, born in Cummington, and married Freedom Whitman, a Baptist clergyman.

Elizabeth Ford, daughter of Andrew and Maria Beal Ford, born in Cummington, and married Stephen Worthington.

Matilda Ford, daughter of Andrew and Maria Beal Ford, born in Cummington, and married Jason Oles, of Goshen, Mass. He was a Presbyterian clergyman, and settled in Hamilton, N. Y.

Jerusha Ford, daughter of Andrew and Maria Beal Ford, born in Cummington, and married and moved to Ohio.

Elijah Fay married Margaret Robinson, daughter of James and Jerusha Bartlet Robinson, and settled in Hamilton, Madison county, N. Y., and he and his wife died there, leaving a son, James, who remained on the homestead, and married Maria Nash, by whom he had a numerous family.

Elias Ford, son of Andrew and Maria Beal Ford, born in Cummington, and Sophia Johnson, daughter of William and Jane Robinson Johnson, died in North Adams, 1838.

His children were : Elias, Sophia, Maria, Polly, Sarah, William C., Jane M., and Clynthia.

ELIAS FORD, son of Elias and Sophia Johnson Ford, born in Hawley, Mass., and married to Ann T. Snyder, of Hillsdale, N. Y., by whom he has two sons : Benjamin and James.

SOPHIA FORD, daughter of Elias and Sophia Johnson Ford, born in Hawley, and married Noah Ford.

MARIA FORD, daughter of Elias and Sophia Ford, born in Hawley, and married to Isaac Atkins.

POLLY FORD, daughter of Elias and Sophia Johnson Ford, born in Hawley, and married to Sherbil Bradford.

SARAH FORD, daughter of Elias and Sophia Johnson Ford, born in Hawley, and married William Temple.

WILLIAM C. FORD, son of Elias and Sophia Johnson Ford, born in Hawley, and married Delia Demmin, 1838, and lives in Fair Haven, Conn.

JANE M. FORD, daughter of Elias and Sophia Johnson Ford, born in Hawley, and died in early life.

CLYNTHIA FORD, daughter of Elias and Sophia Johnson Ford, born in Hawley, and married Mr. Martin, and settled in Minnesota ; died in 1872.

SEYMOUR FOSTER, son of Parla and Phebe Wells Foster, born in Hillsdale, and married Sarah Madeline Truesdell, daughter of the Rev. Harvey and Clynthia Johnson Truesdell, February 20th, 1830; died 1871. His children were: Wells, Henrietta, Augusta and Willie. Wells died in boyhood.

HENRIETTA FOSTER, daughter of Seymour and Sarah Madeline Truesdell Foster, born in Hillsdale, and married Dr. Horace G. Westlake. She has one daughter, Henrietta.

AUGUSTA FOSTER, daughter of Seymour and Sarah Madeline Truesdell Foster, born in Hillsdale, and married to Loring Bartlet, of the city of New York.

MOSES FOSTER, son of Parla and Phebe Wells Foster, born in Hillsdale, and married Esther Sherwood, daughter of Squire and Hannah Collin Sherwood, and settled in Unadilla, Otsego county. N. Y., where he died.

ISAAC FOSTER, son of Parla and Phebe Wells Foster, born in Hillsdale, and married Lucy Sherwood, daughter of Squire and Hannah Collin Sherwood, by whom he had one daughter, Adeline. After the decease of his wife, Lucy, he married Polly Pixley, daughter of John and Anna Sturgis Pixley, by whom he had one daughter, Jane, After the decease of his wife, Polly, he married Nancy Johnson Gerry, widow of Ebenezer Gerry. After the decease of his wife, Nancy, he married Eveline Johnson, daughter of Lemuel Johnson, late of Hillsdale, deceased.

PARLA FOSTER, born in Connecticut, and married Phebe Wells, and settled in Hillsdale, N. Y., in which place he resided many years, and died at a very advanced age. He was a soldier in the war of the revolution, and was a highly esteemed citizen. His children were: Talcott Anna, Moses, Simeon, Isaac, Ely, Deidama, Sally, Katy, Seymour, Judson, and Phebe.

Of the children of Parla Foster, Talcott died early. Emma married Dr. John Esmond, and after his decease she married a Mr. Northrop, and after his decease she married Benjamin Snyder. Moses married Esther Sherwood; Simon married Emily Nichols; Isaac married Lucy Sher-

wood, and after her decease he married Polly Pixley, and
after her decease he married Nancy Garry, and after her
decease he married Emeline Johnson; Eby married Polly
Bushnell; Deidama married Dr. John Stevens; Sally married
Richard Latting; Katy married Stephen Bosworth; Seymour married Sarah Madeline Truesdell; Judson married
Sabrina Messenger, and Phebe married George Woodin.

SYLVESTER C. GARDNER, of Manlius, N, Y., born March
24th, 1811, and married Caroline Collin, daughter of David
and Anna Smith Collin, September 25th, 1838. His children are :

> Edmund, born June 20th, 1840; died June 21st, 1840.
> Caroline, born January 16th, 1842.
> Sylvester, born, November 18th, 1844.
> Sarah, born January 21st, 1849.
> Anna, born December 11th, 1850.
> Miriam, born September 6th, 1852.
> William, born March 26th, 1861.

FRANCIS GODFREY was one of the early settlers of
Bridgewater, Mass., and lived to an advanced age, and
died in 1868. His daughter Elizabeth married John Cary,
one of the first proprietors of that town, and by his will
he appears to have been the grandson of John Cary, of
Somersetshire, England.

JOHN E. GAVIT, born in the city of New York, October
29th, 1817 and was educated in bank note engraving by
his step-father, who was one of the firm of Casilear, Du-
rand & Edmonds. He went to reside in Albany, October,
1836, and on the 28th of November, 1840, married Margaret Sophia Robinson, daughter of Dr. Gain and Chloe
Bradish Robinson. Their children are :

John, born August 4th, 1841; died a few months after.
Joseph, born December 22d, 1842.
Margaret, born March 22d, 1845.
William Edmonds, born February 10th, 1848.
Hellen Elizabeth, born November 26th, 1849.
Clark, born June 27th, 1851.
Julia Niles, born February 22d, 1854.
Chloe, born April 29th, 1856.
Pauline, born February 3d, 1859.

JOSEPH GAVIT, son of John E. and Margaret Sophia
Robinson Gavit, born in Albany, December 22d, 1842, and
married Fanny Palmer, daughter of E. D. Palmer, the celebrated American sculptor. He has one son—John, born
in Albany, July 1st, 1868.

MARGARET GAVIT, daughter of John E. and Margaret
Sophia Robinson Gavit, born in Albany, March 22d, 1845,
and married to Charles Prentis Adams, son of Dr. L. S.
Adams, of Stockbridge, Mass., October 8th, 1868.

JAMES H. GILRUTH, a clergyman and member of the
Iowa Conference of the Methodist Episcopal Church, and
married Sarah Adeline Collin, daughter of Henry A. and
Sarah Ann White Collin, of Mount Vernon, Linn county,
Iowa, June 20th, 1869. They have one daughter, born
March 1st, 1870.

PHILIP GRANDIN, married Amanda Robinson, daughter
of Gain and Chloe Bradish Robinson, by whom he has had
eleven children, only two of whom are now living. His son
William graduated at West Point. And two of his sons
were twins, one of whom was named Andrew Jackson, and
the other Martin Van Buren.

WILLIAM HANLEY, born in Virginia, April 17th, 1833,
and married Melind T. Wright, daughter of Lewis and

Hannah Collin Wright, November 27th, 1857 ; died August 5th, 1870.   His children are :

Marislin, born August 16th, 1859.
John Collin, born November 30th, 1861.
Louis Wright, born November 2d, 1863.
William Alonzo, born December 12th, 1865.

EBENEZER HAMLINE, grand father of the Rev. Leonidas Lent Hamline, was born in Middletown, Conn., 1740, and married Lois Brooks, and settled in Burlington, Conn. ; died in 1810.   He had six children : Mark, Daniel, Lent, Rosa, Hannah, and Lois.   He was a soldier in the French war, and an officer in the war of the revolution.

DANIEL HAMLINE, son of Ebenezer and Lois Brooks Hamline, married Lucretia Barns, and settled in Saratoga county, N. Y.   They had a large family of children.

LENT HAMLINE, son of Ebenezer and Lois Brooks Hamline, settled in New London, Conn., and died there.

ROSA HAMLINE, daughther of Ebenezer and Lois Brooks Hamline, married and settled in Burlington, Conn., and died there.

HANNAH HAMLINE, daughter of Ebenezer and Lois Brooks Hamline, married Thomas Beckwith, and died in Burlington, Conn.

LOIS HAMLINE, daughter of Ebenezer and Lois Brooks Hamline, died in Canton, Conn., at a very advanced age.

MARK HAMLINE, son of Ebenezer and Lois Brooks Hamline, born in Burlington, Conn., 1763, and married Roxana Moses, daughter of Othneal Moses ; died in 1840. They had ten children, two of whom died in infancy.   The survivors were : Philo, Leonidas, Lent, Norman, Roxana,

Experience, Saphrona, Harriet, and Hannah. His wife Roxana died at Canton, Conn., 1831, and he married Deidama Humphry, widow of Judge James Humphry, of Canton.

PHILO HAMLINE, son of Mark and Roxana Moses Hamline, married Thurza Barber, and settled in New Hartford, Connecticut, and had eleven children. He was born 1788 ; died 1857. His wife, Thurza, died in canton 1851. One of their daughters (Mariette) married Hiram Foster, a farmer of Mendon, Massachusetts, and had three sons, all of whom volunteered as soldiers in the late civil war, and one of whom died from neglect and ill treatment in the hospital in the city of Washington, D. C.

NORMAN HAMLINE, son of Mark and Roxana Moses Hamline, died in some of the southern States.

ROXANA HAMLINE, daughter of Mark and Roxana Moses Hamline, married Friend White, of Hartford county, Connecticut, and died leaving several children.

SOPHRONA HAMLINE, daughter of Mark and Roxana Moses Hamline, married David Humphrey, of Great Barrington, Massachusetts, and died in 1847, leaving six children.

EXPERIENCE HAMLINE, daughter of Mark and Roxana Moses Hamline, married Mr. Billings, and died in 1857. Her husband died in Indiana, 1855.

HARRIET HAMLINE, daughter of Mark and Roxana Moses Hamline, married Zelotes Mather, and after his death married Isaac J. Bigelow, December 10th, 1838.

HANNAH HAMLINE, daughter of Mark and Roxana Moses Hamline, married Rev. James Longhead, who settled in Morris, Illinois.

LEONIDAS LENT HAMLINE, son of Mark and Roxana Moses Hamline, born in Hartford county, Connecticut, May 10th, 1797. He was educated for the ministry, but suspended his studies on account of ill health. He subsequently studied law. On the 6th of March, 1824, he married Eliza Price, daughter of Jeffrey Price, of Zanesville, Ohio. He subsequently become a minister of the Methodist Episcopal Church, and joined the Ohio Conference in 1832. His wife, Eliza, died in Cincinnati, March 27th, 1835, leaving one son, Leonidas Price. In 1836 he married Melinda Johnson Truesdell, widow of Arnold Truesdell, and daughter of William and Jane Robinson Johnson. In 1836 he was appointed Editor of the *Western Christian Advocate*, associated with the Rev. Charles Elliot. In 1840 was appointed Editor of the *Ladies' Magazine*, published at Cincinnati, Ohio. In 1844 he was elected a Bishop of the Methodist Episcopal Church, in which capacity he labored till his health failed in 1852, when he resigned that position and died at Mount Pleasant, Henry county, Iowa, March 23d, 1865. He was buried at Evanston, Illinois, where a Scotch granite monument is erected to his memory. He had a commanding appearance, a gentlemanly address, and possessed talents and eloquence of a high order.

LEONIDAS PRICE HAMLINE, son of Leonidas Lent and Eliza Price Hamline, born in Zanesville, Ohio, August 13th, 1829. He graduated at the Medical College at Castleton, Vermont, and married Virginia Moore, daughter of Capt. John Moore, of Peoria, Illinois, December 31st, 1850. They have had five children :

Leonidas Moore, born October 5th, 1852.
John Henry, born March 23d, 1856.
Eliza, born February 6th, 1859; died February 26th, 1859.

Theodosia, born June 30th, 1862.

Virginia Malinda, born March 23d, 1866.

LYDIA HAMLINE, born in Dutchess county, March 30th, 1783, and married James Collin, son of David and Esther Gillett Collin, April 21st, 1804; died November 1st, 1855. Her children were :

Ely, born February 23d, 1805.

James Hamblin, born March 5th, 1808.

Lydia Louise, born June 15th, 1810.

Julia Ann, born November 17th, 1813.

Caroline, born September 21st, 1817.

Cordelia, born April 6th, 1820.

Aulia, born April 6th, 1820; died April 6th, 1820.

David Nelson, born March 17th, 1823; died March 3d, 1840.

LEMUEL HILL, born 1751, died August 25th, 1828. His father and two brothers came from Old and settled in New England. Among his children were two sons, Jonathan and Harvey.

JONATHAN HILL, son of Lemuel Hill, born March 4th, 1775, and married Chastine E. Wilcox, February 25th, 1801. Their children were :

Rodney, born January 27th, 1802.

Sibyl Vilona, born October 24th, 1803.

Pluma A., born December 26th, 1805.

Cornelia E., born March 16th, 1808.

Alice C., born February 3d, 1810.

John, born May 1st, 1812.

Henry L., born February 2d, 1816.

Chastine E., born July 22d, 1819.

RODNEY HILL, son of Jonathan and Chastine E. Wilcox Hill, born January 27th, 1802, and married Sarah Amanda

Collin, daughter of John and Ruth Holman Johnson Collin, February 20th, 1825. Their children are :

John Henry, born May 10th, 1826.
Ruth Maria, born January 23d, 1829.

JOHN HENRY HILL, son of Rodney and Sarah A. Collin Hill, born May 10th, 1826, and married Catharine Augusta Hull, June 3d, 1850. Their children are :

Rodney, born November 6th, 1852.
John Henry, born October 28th, 1854.
John Edward, born December 13th, 1857.
Frank Albert, born February 8th, 1860.
Fred Augustus, born February 6th, 1861.
Charles Pomeroy, born September 1st, 1863.

PLUMER A. HILL, daughter of Jonathan and Chastine E. Wilcox Hill, born December 26th, 1805, and married Albert Winslow, of Hillsdale, and died at Monterey, Mass.

SIBYL VELONA HILL, daughter of Jonathan and Chastine E. Wilcox Hill, born October 24th, 1803, and married James Collin, son of John and Ruth Holman Johnson Collin, March 17th, 1828; died August 11th, 1846. Her children are :

Ellen H., born February 20th, 1829.
Charles R., born March 1st, 1832.
Louis E., born August 10th, 1833.
John H., born February 25th, 1835.
Mary C., born March 15th, 1838.
William M., born March 23d, 1842.

CORNELIA E. HILL, daughter of Jonathan and Chastine E. Wilcox Hill, born March 16th, 1808, and married Henry Williams, of Alford, Mass., and settled in Dayton, Ohio.

ALICE C. HILL, daughter of Jonathan and Chastine E. Hill, born February 3d, 1810, and married Collins Hunt, of Lenox, Mass.

JOHN HILL, son of Jonathan and Chastine E. Wilcox Hill, born May 1st, 1812, and married Miss Wilcox, and died in Chicago, Illinois.

HENRY L. HILL, son of Jonathan and Chastine E. Wilcox Hill, born February 2d, 1816, has been twice married, and is settled in Chicago, Illinois.

CHASTINE E. HILL, daughter of Jonathan and Chastine E. Wilcox Hill, born July 22d, 1819, and married Mr. Garfield, of Monterey, Mass.

THOMAS HOLMAN and ABIGAIL his wife, resided in Milton, Mass., and had ten children. He was selectman and town clerk.

Abigail, born February 15th, 1665.
Nana, born September 15th, 1668.
Patience, born February 24th, 1670.
Sarah, born April 13th, 1673.
Mary, born March 8th, 1674; died June 4th, 1675; and Thomas, born March 8th, 1674, twins.
Mary, born August 24th, 1677.
John, born March 13th, 1679.
Ann, born August 11th, 1680.
Samuel, born June 27th, 1683.

NANA HOLMAN, daughter of Thomas and Abigail Holman, born September 15th, 1668, and married Benjamin Beal, of Braintree, June 17th, 1700.

SARAH HOLMAN, daughter of Thomas and Abigail Holman, born April 13th, 1673, and married Richard Woods, of Boston, October 9th, 1701.

ANN HOLMAN, daughter of Thomas and Abigail Holman, born August 11th, 1680, and married Samuel Swift, of Milton, Mass., November 6th, 1707.

JOHN HOLMAN, son of Thomas and Abigail Holman, born in Milton, Mass., March 13th, 1679, graduated at the Harvard University, 1700, and married Ann, the daughter of Daniel Quincy, of Boston, and sister of John Quincy, of Braintree, Mass.; died 1759. He was a colonel in the State militia, and a Representative in the Massachusetts Legislature in the years 1734–1737 and 1744, in which capacity, as well as in all others, he was highly respected. His children were : John, Ann, Peggy, Ruth and Mary.

JOHN HOLMAN, son of John and Ann Quincy Holman, born in Bridgewater, Mass., and married Ann, daughter of Isaac Harris, 1734 ; died 1755. His wife died 1757, aged 45 years. He was a captain in the State militia. His children were :

Sarah, born 1736.
Ann, born 1738.
William, born 1740.
Abigail, born 1743.
Isaac and Jane.

ANN HOLMAN, daughter of John and Ann Quincy Holman, married Joseph Billings, of Stoughton, Mass., 1730.

PEGGY HOLMAN, daughter of John and Ann Quincy Holman, married John Johnson, son of Isaac and Abigail Johnson, 1731.

RUTH HOLMAN, daughter of John and Ann Quincy Holman, married Benjamin Johnson, 6th son of Isaac Johnson, and grandfather of Ruth Holman Johnson Collin, 1732.

MARY HOLMAN, daughter of John and Ann Quincy Holman, married Ezra Cary, 1737. Their children were:

Sarah, born, 1738; and Shepherd, born 1742.

JANE HOLMAN, daughter of John and Ann Harris Holman, married Ephraim Cary, 1771. Their children were:

Jane, born 1773.
Salome, born 1774.
Cyrus, born 1777.
William Holman, born 1779.
Ephraim, born 1782.
Shepherd, born 1784.
Susanna, born 1787.
Francis, born 1789.
Jason, born 1791.
Asnath, born 1793.
Harmony, born 1796.

EDWARD B. HUNT, son of Samuel and Sally Bagley Hunt, born in Hillsdale, February, 15, 1814, and married Susan Burtis, daughter of Thomas Burtis, February 2d, 1857. After the death of his wife, Susan, he married Eliza Esmond, daughter of Spencer and Sally Sherwood Esmond, September 19th, 1866.

EMMA HOUSE, daughter of Benjamin and Phebe Vanderburgh House, born in Hillsdale, November 7th, 1820, and married Elisha W. Bushnell, son of John and Loxey Lay Bushnell, September 1st, 1840 ; died November 16th, 1859. Her children were :

Sarah, born November 7th, 1841.
George House, born August 14th, 1843 ; died March 7th, 1845.
Mary Vanderburgh, born April 20th, 1847 ; died May 3d, 1848.

George Vanderburgh, born September 11th, 1851.
Clayton, born October 23d, 1857; died November 21st, 1859.

Jane B. Hunt, daughter of Benjamin Hunt, of Lenox, Mass., born June 22d, 1801, and married James Collin, son of John and Ruth Holman Johnson Collin, May 5th, 1822; died February 25th, 1827. Her children were:

James H., born March 21st, 1823.
Jane S., born November 27th, 1824.
John Francis, born February 15th, 1827; died April 29th, 1828.

Rhoda How, of Connecticut, married Bentley White, March 3d, 1819; died April 14th, 1841. Her children were:

Sarah Ann, born January 14th, 1820.
Sibyl M., born May 29th, 1822; died December 18th, 1824.
Stephen, born March 17th, 1826.
Jane M., born October 20th, 1832; died October 20th, 1834.

Edward Johnson, born, Horn Hill, Kent, England, 1599; died at Woburn, Mass., April 23d, 1672. He came to this country with Gov. Winthrop, 1630, and was prominent in the organization of the town and church of Woburn, 1642. Was a captain of its military company; was chosen its representative in 1643. and annually re-elected until 1671; was speaker of the house, 1665, and was on the committee with Broadstreet, Danforth and others, to meet the Commissioners Nicolls, Carr, etc., who had been sent from England. He was recorder of the town from its incorporation till his death. Some of his writings were published in London, in 1654, and reprinted in the Massachusetts

Historical Collections, and again with notes, by W. F. Poole, in 1867.

ISAAC JOHNSON, one of the founders of Massachusetts, born in Clipsham, Rutlandshire, England; died in Boston, September 30th, 1630. He came over with Gov. Winthrop, arriving at Salem, June 12th, 1630. He was one of the four who founded the first church at Charlestown, July 30th and September 7th; he conducted the first settlement of Boston. He was a good and a wise man, and was the wealthiest of the colonists. Arabella, his wife, was the daughter of Thomas, the fourteenth Earl of Lincoln. She accompanied her husband to New England, and died in Salem, August 30th, 1630. In honor of her, the name of the *Eagle*, Winthrop's ship, was changed to the *Arabella*.

ISAAC JOHNSON, of Hingham, Mass., born 1668, and married Abigail, widow of Isaac Lazell, and daughter of John Leavitt; died 1730. He was a captain, a magistrate and four years a representative in the Massachusetts Legislature. It is a well authenticated tradition that his grandfather emigrated to this country with Gov. Winthrop in 1630; and it is therefore a fair conclusion that his grandfather was either Edward or Isaac Johnson, who did accompany Gov. Winthrop. His children were:

David, Solomon, Daniel, James, Deborah.
Sarah, born 1702.
John, born 1705.
Joseph, born 1707.
Benjamin, born 1711, and
Mary, born 1716.

Captain DAVID JOHNSON, son of Isaac and Abigail John-son, married Rebecca, daughter of John Washburn, 1719. Their children were:

Isaac, born 1721.
David, born 1724.
Mary, born 1729.
Sarah, born 1732, and
Rebecca, born 1734.

SOLOMON JOHNSON, son of Isaac and Abigail Johnson, married Susanna, daughter of Joseph Edson, 1723 ; died 1771. Their children were :

Susanna, born 1723.
Seth, born 1733.
Josiah, born 1735.
Nathan, born 1738.
Mary, born 1740.

Judge DANIEL JOHNSON, son of Isaac and Abigail Johnson, married Betty, daughter of James Latham, 1720 ; died 1741. His children were :

James, born 1728.
Jeremiah, born 1734.
Leavitt, born 1736.

The great grandmother of Betty Latham was the famous Mary Chilton, who was the first female that set foot on Plymouth shore in 1620.

DANIEL JOHNSON, son of Judge Daniel and Betty Latham Johnson, graduated at the Harvard University 1767, and settled in the ministry at Harvard 1769, and died their September 23d, 1777.

JOSIAH JOHNSON, son of Judge Daniel and Betty Latham Johnson. married Ruth, daughter of Eliphalet Leonard, 1757. Their children were, James, Daniel, Cyrus, Ruth and Betty.

James married Sally Washburn, and settled in Easton,

Maine. Daniel married Mary·Barker, and settled in the city of New York as an attorney. Cyrus was a physician, and married Henrietta, daughter of Deacon Isaac Lazell.

JOSIAH JOHNSON, son of Solomon and Susannah Edson Johnson, married Azuba, daughter of Ephraim Cary; died 1812. She died 1816. They had only one child, Solomon, who married Sally, daughter of Gain Robinson, and settled in Rhode Island.

MAJ. JOHN JOHNSON, son of Isaac and Abigail Johnson, married Peggy, daughter of John and Ann Quincy Holman, 1731; died 1770. She died 1757. Their children were :

Sarah, born 1733.
Abial, born 1735.
Lewis, born 1738.
Patience, born 1744.
Joseph, born 1747.
Content, born 1748.
Calvin, born 1751.

BENJAMIN JOHNSON, son of Isaac and Abigail Johnson, married Ruth, daughter of John and Ann Quincy Holman, 1732; died 1768. She died 1764. Their children were :

Ruth, born 1736.
Benjamin, born 1739.
Rhoda, born 1743,
William, born 1753.

Ruth married Stephen Richardson. Benjamin died in the army. Rhoda married Winslow Richardson.

WILLIAM JOHNSON, son of Benjamin and Ruth Holman Johnson, born in Bridgwater, Mass., 1753, and married Jane Robinson, daughter of James and Jerusha Bartlet

Robinson, 1779; died at Hillsdale, April, 1818. His children were :

Ruth Holman, born September 16th, 1780.
Sophia, born January 7th, 1784.
Melinda, born December 7th, 1785 ; died March 9th, 1792.
Clynthia, born April 7th, 1788.
Quincy, born April 5th, 1791.
Melinda, born September 29th, 1801.

RUTH HOLMAN JOHNSON, daughter of William and Jane Robinson Johnson, born in Bridgwater, Mass., September 16th, 1780, and married John Collin, son of John and Sarah Arnold Collin, of Hillsdale, N. Y., October 23d, 1798 ; died in Hillsdale, December 2d, 1868. Her children were :

James, born January 16th, 1800.
John Francis, born April 30th, 1802.
Sarah Amanda, born April 21st, 1804.
Jane Miranda, born February 14th, 1807.
Hannah, born December 19th, 1809.
Ruth Maria, born March 1st, 1813 ; died May, 1838.
Henry Augustus, born January 6th, 1817.
William Quincy, born November 23d, 1819; died July 30th, 1822.
Clynthia A., born December 10th, 1822 ; died August 5th, 1828.

SOPHIA JOHNSON, daughter of William and Jane Robinson Johnson, born in Cummington, Mass., January 7th, 1784, and married Elias Ford, son of Andrew and Maria Beal Ford, and settled in Hawley, Mass. She died in 1831. Her children were : Elias, Sophia, Maria Polly, Sarah, William C., Jane M., and Clynthia.

MELINDA JOHNSON, daughter of William and Jane Robinson Johnson, born in Cummington, Mass., December 7th, 1785 ; died March 9th, 1792.

CLYNTHIA JOHNSON, daughter of William and Jane Robinson Johnson. born in Cummington, Mass., April 7th, 1788, and married Rev. Harry Truesdell, son of Thomas and Hannah Collin Truesdell, February 9th, 1809. Her children are :

Arnold Fletcher, born January 6th, 1810.
Sarah Madaline, born May 12th, 1812.
John Quincy, born February 22d, 1825.

QUINCY JOHNSON, son of Wilborn and Jane Robinson Johnson, born in Cummington, Mass., April 5th, 1791, and married Abigail Cook, of Otis, Mass., May, 1812. His children were :

Wesley, born February 24th, 1813; died July 1st, 1844.
Marvin, born December 16th, 1814; died September 20th, 1841.
William Leonard, born September 5th, 1816.
Jane, born April 24th, 1818; died November 24th, 1830.
John Quincy, born August 28th, 1822.
Melinda, born December 31st, 1823.
James Leroy, born April 17th, 1822; died 1869.

After the death of his wife Abigail, he married Mrs. Eveline, widow of Capt. Isaac Foster, and daughter of Lemuel Johnson, late of Hillsdale, deceased.

MELINDA JOHNSON, daughter of William and Jane Robinson Johnson, born September 29th, 1801, and married Arnold Truesdell, son of Thomas and Hannah Collin Truesdell, September 10th, 1820. He died at Wilmington, Ohio, March 28th, 1835, and she married Rev. Leonidas L. Hamline, of Cincinnati, Ohio, 1836. He subsequently became a Bishop of the Methodist Episcopal church, and after years devoted to his duties in that capacity, he retired to his estate in Mount Pleasant, Iowa, where he died March 23d, 1865, leaving a large estate to his wife and son. She now resides at Everston, Illinois.

WESLEY JOHNSON, son of Quincy and Abigail Cook Johnson, born in Hillsdale, February 24th, 1813. He spent several years in Africa, assisting in the foundation of the colony in Liberia. He went as physician to the Governor's family, and subsequently discharged the duties of Governor himself. He was once wounded in repelling an attack of the natives upon the colony. He devoted time and money in the establishment of a college there, and finally fell a victim to the malaria of the climate. After suffering with African fever, he returned to his home in America, ardently desiring a restoration to health that he might complete the enterprises he had commenced for the benefit of the colony. But the seeds of death had been sown, and he died in Hillsdale, July 1st, 1844, universally respected for his talents, scholarship, enterprise, and amiable characteristics.

MARVIN JOHNSON, son of Quincy and Abigail Cook Johnson, born in Hillsdale, December 16th, 1814, and married Miss Park, of Chatham, N. Y.; died September 2d, 1841.

WILLIAM LEONARD JOHNSON, son of Quincy and Abigail Cook Johnson, born in Hillsdale, September 5th, 1816, and married Emeline Sornborger, September 12th, 1852. Their children were :

Ida, born September 10th, 1853; died April 24th, 1856.
Willie, born September 13th, 1855; died September 25th, 1855.
Franklin, born June 2d, 1857.
George Quincy, born December 5th, 1859.

JANE JOHNSON, daughter of Quincy and Abigail Cook Johnson, born in Hillsdale, April 24th, 1818; died November 24th, 1830.

JOHN QUINCY JOHNSON, son of Quincy and Abigail Cook Johnson, born in Hillsdale, August 28th, 1820, and married Sally Latting, daughter of Richard and Sally Foster Latting, March 24th, 1844. Their children are :

Wesley R., born January 6th, 1845.

Jane M., born February 4th, 1847.

Hiram W., born January 23d, 1849.

Parla, born December 12th, 1850.

Lillia E., born August 14th, 1855.

Quincy, born July 22d, 1857.

Theophilus, born November 18th, 1859.

JAMES LEROY JOHNSON, son of Quincy and Abigail Cook Johnson, born in Hillsdale, April 17th, 1822 ; died in Missouri, 1869.

MELINDA JOHNSON, daughter of Quincy and Abigail Cook Johnson, born in Hillsdale, December 31st, 1823.

ARTEMAS JOHNSON, son of Lemuel Johnson, born January 20th, 1785, and married Susan Sherwood, daughter of Squire and Hannah Collin Sherwood, February 12th, 1814; died December 13th, 1865. Their children were :

Julia, born August 31st, 1815 ; died March 22d, 1859.

Mary, born March 21st, 1818 ; died April 18th, 1869.

Nancy, born August 31st, 1820; died September 10th, 1848.

Parker, born June 18th, 1822.

LeRoy, born April 22d, 1824; died September 17th, 1827.

Henry, born May 27th, 1826; died August 15th, 1869.

Jane, born April 30th, 1828.

Lee, born July 29th, 1831.

Dwight, born January 31st, 1833.

Artemas, born July 31st, 1836; died September 13th, 1841.

Lucy, born October 3d, 1839; died September 16th, 1841.

BETTY LATHAM, daughter of James Latham, and granddaughter of Robert Latham, and great great grandaughter of the famous Mary Chilton, who was the first female to set foot on Plymouth shore, in 1620, was born in Bridgwater, Mass., and married to Judge Daniel Johnson, son of Isaac and Abigail Johnson, 1726. Her kinsman, William Latham, born in 1803, and graduated at Brown's University in 1827, and settled in South Bridgwater as an attorney, is a descendant in the fifth degree from Robert and Susan Winslow Latham ; and I am indebted to his kindness for much information contained in these pages.

CHARLES MEAD, of Dutchess county, N. Y., married Caroline Collin, daughter of James and Lydia Hamblin Collin, April 3d, 1840. Their children were :

Charles Nelson, born April 23d, 1841 ; died July 11th, 1850.

James Arthur, born March 2d, 1843.

Caroline E., born March 2d, 1845.

Martha, born May 25th, 1847.

Clara B., born December 11th, 1849.

Ellen, born May 22d, 1852.

Robert Collin, born July 28th, 1857.

Carl Fremont, born November 5th, 1860.

Frederick Mesick, born in Claverack, and married Harriet Collin, daughter of David and Lucy Bingham Collin, March 3d, 1823. She died February 28th, 1826, and he subsequently married Joanna Latting, daughter of Refine Latting, of Hillsdale, by whom he had several children. After the death of his wife Joanna, he married a Mrs. Jarvis, and died in Claverack.

Miles Merwin, born in England or Wales, in 1623, emigrated to this country in 1645, and became the owner of a large tract of land situated on Long Island sound, and now known as Pond Point or Merwin's Point. It was mostly situated in the town of Milford, New Haven county, Conn., but extended easterly across Oyster river into what is now the town of Orange. By Lambert's history of Milford, it appears that he was a tanner and currier, and also engaged in commerce, being part owner of two brigs and a sloop, the latter employed in coasting while the former made voyages to the West Indies. He died April 3d, 1697. By his first wife he had the following children:

Eliza.
John, born 1650.
Abigail.
Thomas.
Samuel, born August 21st, 1656.
Miles, born December 14th, 1658.
Daniel, born 1661.

His first wife having died, 1664, he married the widow of Thomas Beach, by whom he had the following children: Martha and Mary, twins, born January 23d, 1666; Hannah, born 1667; and Deborah, born 1670, at which time his second wife died. His first wife joined the Congregational Church, June 2d, 1661, and he joined the same church in the November following.

His daughter Eliza married Mr. Canfield.
Abigail married Abel Holbrook.
Deborah married Mr. Burwell.
Daniel died young.
Samuel married Sarah Woodin.
Thomas settled in Norwalk.

JOHN MERWIN, son of Miles Merwin, by his first marriage, was born in Milford, 1650. He settled on the homestead. His wife's name was Mary. His children were:

John, born, 1680.
Joseph and Hannah.
John was baptized, 1682, Joseph, in 1686, and Hannah, in 1690.

JOHN MERWIN, son of John and Mary Merwin, born in Milford, 1680, and settled on the homestead. His wife's name was Hannah. His children were:

John, born, 1707.
Hannah, born 1708.
Joseph, Sarah and David.

His wife Hannah joined the First Congregational Church of Milford on the 22d of May, 1720, and his five children were baptized on the same day.

JOHN MERWIN, son of John and Hannah Merwin, born in Milford, 1707; died February 19th, 1792. His children were: Elizabeth, John and Daniel.

HANNAH MERWIN, daughter of John and Hannah Merwin, born in Milford, 1708, and married John Collin, an emigrant from France, 1730. Her children were:

John, born 1732.
David, born 1734.
James, born 1736; died in his infancy.

DAVID MERWIN, son of John Merwin 3d, born in Milford, and married Eunice Perry, by whom he had several children, among whom were John, Isaac David, Merrit, and Mark.

JOHN MERWIN, son of John Merwin 3d, and grandson of John and Hannah Merwin, born in Milford, March, 1735, and married Elizabeth Buckingham, 1755; died, 1826. His children were: John, Elizabeth, Content, Sarah, Samuel, and Daniel.

SAMUEL MERWIN, son of John and Elizabeth Buckingham Merwin, born in Milford, 1775, and married Susan Nettleton, 1795, by whom he had a daughter—Sarah. After the death of his wife Susan, he married Mary Welch, September, 1800, by whom he had seven children: Susan, Mary, Caroline, John Welch, Samuel Orange, Homer, and Markus.

SUSAN MARY MERWIN, daughter of Samuel and Mary Welch Merwin, born in Milford, 1801, and married to Sidney Buckingham, January, 1825. Their children were:

Lucy Belden, born June 6th, 1832; died September, 1833.
Charles Augustus, born June, 1838; died October, 1849.
She has given important assistance in this compilation.

CAROLINE MERWIN, daughter of Samuel and Mary Welch Merwin, born in Milford, 1803, and married to Charles Pond Strong, March, 1825; died, 1836. She had two children:

Charles William, born March, 1833.
Caroline Merwin, born March, 1836.

JOHN WELCH MERWIN, son of Samuel and Mary Welch Merwin, born 1807, and married to Rebecca Louise Huntington, 1840, and had one child, John Huntington, born 1842. After the decease of his wife, Rebecca Louise, he married Maria Gilbert Huntington, by whom he had five children :

Maria Louise, born January, 1847.
Edward Gilbert, born November 1848.
George Henry, born 1850.
Charles Augustus, born 1852.
William Albert, born 1856.

SAMUEL ORANGE MERWIN, son of Samuel and Mary
• Welch Merwin, born March, 1810, and married Susan T. Chapman, of Virginia, 1833 ; died 1865. His children were : John, Caroline, Virginia, William Frederick, Mary, Charles Buckingham, Samuel, Josephine, and Charlotte.

HOMER MERWIN, son of Samuel and Mary Welch Merwin, born July, 1812 ; died November, 1840.

CHARLES MERWIN, son of Samuel and Mary Welch Merwin, born 1805, and married Aurelia C. Platt, January 4th, 1827 ; died December 19th, 1867. His children were :

George Platt, born October 16th, 1828.
Mary Susan, born October 5th, 1830.
Samuel Clark, born March 22d, 1833.
William Henry, born August 15th, 1835.
John Welch, born January 10th, 1838.
Caroline Elizabeth, born January 5th, 1841.
Charles Homer, born September 30th, 1843.

MILES MERWIN, son of Miles and Mary Briscoe Merwin, and great grandson of John and Mary Merwin, born at the homestead (Merwin's Point), 1750, and married to

Abigail Ann Beach, and settled at Merwin's Point; died 1820. His children were :

Miles, born 1774.

Abigail Ann, born 1771.

Daniel, born 1779.

Samuel, born 1782.

Mary, born 1785.

Anson, born 1788.

Nathan, born 1791.

Benedict, born 1794.

STEPHEN MERWIN, son of Miles and Mary Briscoe Merwin, born at Merwin's Point, and settled in Milford, where he married and had three children : David, Stephen, and Huldah.

SAMUEL MERWIN, son of Miles and Mary Briscoe Merwin, born at Merwin's Point, and never married.

MARY MERWIN, daughter of Miles and Mary Briscoe Merwin, born at Merwin's Point, and married Jeremiah Platt, and settled in Bridgeport. Connecticut.

HULDAH MERWIN, daughter of Miles and Mary Briscoe Merwin, born at Merwin's Point, and married Eli Smith, and settled in Bridgeport, Connecticut.

MILES MERWIN, son of Miles and Abigail Ann Beach Merwin, born at Merwin's Point, 1774, and married Julia Carrington, 1800; died in Milford, 1846.

ABIGAIL ANN MERWIN, daughter of Miles and Abigail Ann Beach Merwin, born at Merwin's Point, 1771, and married Nat. Hepburn, 1795; died in New York city, 1861.

DANIEL MERWIN, son of Miles and Abigail Ann Beach

Merwin, born at Merwin's Point, 1779, and married Mary Tomlinson, 1807; died in Milford, 1858.

SAMUEL MERWIN, son of Miles and Abigail Ann Beach Merwin, born at Milford's Point, 1782, and married Clarina B. Taylor, 1807; died in New Haven, 1856.

MARY MERWIN, daughter of Miles and Abigail Ann Beach Merwin, born at Merwin's Point, 1785, and married Rev. Charles Atwater, 1809, and settled in North Branford, Conn.

ANSON MERWIN, son of Miles and Abigail Ann Merwin, born at Merwin's Point, 1788, and married Calina Tomlinson, 1812; died in Milford, 1868.

NATHAN MERWIN, son of Miles and Abigail Ann Merwin, born at Merwin's Point, 1791, and married Nancy Whiting, 1816.

MARCUS MERWIN, son of Samuel and Mary Welch Merwin, born January 28th, 1817, and married Abigail Martha Smith, February 3d, 1845; she having been born August 18th, 1830. They settled at Merwin's Point, and have had six children:

> Charles Philip, born November 15th, 1845; died February 7th, 1846.
> Charles Philip, born December 6th, 1846.
> Emma Virginia, born February 6th, 1849.
> Homer Smith, born February 9th, 1851.
> Julia Hudson, born April 30th, 1854; died July 4th, 1859.
> Harry Merryman, born March 14th, 1864.

CHARLES PHILIP MERWIN, son of Marcus and Abigail Martha Smith Merwin, born December 6th, 1846, and married Hattie Hitchcock, January, 1871.

JOHN WELCH MERWIN, son of Charles and Anna C. Platt
Merwin, lives on a part of the Merwin's Point farm. He
has no family.

BENEDICT MERWIN, son of Miles and Abigail Ann Beach
Merwin, born 1794, and married Polly Isabel, 1818; died,
1868. He settled at Merwin's Point, or Pond Point.

JESSE MERWIN, son of Daniel Merwin, born in Milford,
Conn., August 25th, 1784, and settled in Kinderhook,
N. Y., where he died November 8th, 1852.

It is a well authenticated fact that Jesse Merwin was
the original of "Ichabod Crane," in a legend of Sleepy
Hollow in Washington Irving's Sketch Book ; they having
made the acquaintance of each other, and Irving having
formed a strong attachment to him while residing in the
family of Judge Van Ness, in Kinderhook. In fact, Jesse
Merwin secured the love and esteem of all who knew him.

He married Jane Van Dyck, October 16th, 1808. His
children were :

Daniel E., born September 1st, 1812 ; died January
5th, 1865.
Henry, born July 16th, 1814 ; died March 28th, 1866.
Catharine, born March 11th, 1816.
Asher, born March 30th, 1818.
Cornelius, born April 30th, 1820 ; died June 30th,
1871.
Albertine, born May 4th, 1822.
Jane E., born December 19th, 1824.
Samuel, born December 12th, 1826.
David, born May 19th, 1829.
W. J., born May 30th, 1834.

W. J. MERWIN, son of Jesse and Jane Van Dyck Merwin, born in Kinderhook, May 30th, 1834, and married

December 3d, 1856, to Mary Reynolds, who was born December 23d, 1831. His children are :

James R., born September 16th, 1857.
Mary A., born August 8th, 1860.
Clarence B., born March 21st, 1862.
Katie, born June 30th, 1865.
Louis, born January 21st, 1868.
Ada, born April 21st, 1871.

The Merwin family having been an important root of the Collin family, has received a somewhat particular attention.

Homogeneous and unique, like the people of New England generally, while participating largely in the great and good characteristics of that people, they have been free from the bigotry and avarice that has characterized too many of them.

One of their interesting characteristics is their attachment to their old ancestral home, it having remained in possession of the family two hundred and twenty-seven years.

Their longevity—many of them living from seventy to ninety years—is, no doubt, the result of wise and temperate habits.

Their high moral characteristics are evinced in the fact that most of them are members, and some of them are clergymen, of the different religious denominations. And, notwithstanding their numbers extending through centuries of the past and over a vast extent of country, all have been chacterized for intelligence, integrity, industry, enterprise and high social dispositions.

REV. ABNER MORSE, born at Medway, Mass., September 5th, 1793 ; died at Sharon, Mass., May 16th, 1865 ; graduated at Brown University, 1816. He was distinguished as a genealogist, and he published a memorial of the Morses, in 1850.

·Rev. Jedediah Morse, born at Woodstock, Conn., August 23d, 1761; died at New Haven, June 9th, 1826. He graduated at Yale College, 1783. He was the first prominent geographer of America. Among his children were :

Samuel Finley Breese, born April 27th, 1791.
Sydney Edwards, born February 7th, 1794.

Samuel Finley Bruce Morse, born April 27th, 1791; died April 2d, 1872. He was the son of the Rev. Jedediah Morse, and graduated at Yale College, 1810. He was distinguished as a portrait painter and statuary, and is immortalized as the author and discoverer of the Electric Telegraph. He edited the poems, with a biographical sketch, of Lucretia Maria Davidson, to whose grandmother, Deidama Morse Collin, he was related.

Sydney Edwards Morse, son of Rev. Jedediah Morse, born at Charlestown, Mass., February 7th, 1794 ; died in New York, December 23d, 1871. He was distinguished as a journalist, and was the author and discoverer of several useful inventions.

Elijah Matson, born October, 1768, and married Sarah Grinell, December, 1796. They had a son, John, born February 3d, 1806, who married Margaret Waterman, September 10th, 1833, whose children were :

Cordelia, born November 22d, 1834.
Alvin, born December 10th, 1836.
Chloe, born May 31st, 1840.
James, born May 25th, 1842.
Lewis, born October 11th, 1844.
Lydia A., born January 12th, 1847.
George T., born January 24th, 1851.
Sarah O., born February 17th, 1853.

CHLOE MATSON, daughter of John and Margaret Waterman Matson, born in Waterloo, Indiana, May 31st, 1840, and married Henry Alonzo Collin, son of Henry Augustus and Sarah Ann White Collin, June 30th, 1868, by whom she has one child, Ruthie, born June 16th, 1869.

DEIDAMA MORSE, sister of Josiah Morse, of Hillsdale, N. Y., born in Connecticut, February 22d, 1748, and married Captain Oliver Davidson, of Canterbury, Conn., 1779; died in Hillsdale, June 9th, 1831. Her children were :

Oliver, born in Canterbury, 1781.
Joseph, born in Canterbury, 1783.
Anna, born in Canterbury, 1785.

After the decease of her husband, Oliver Davidson, and on the 13th of May, 1792, she married Captain John Collin. Her granddaughters, Lucretia Maria and Margaret Miller Davidson, possessed poetic talents of the highest order.

JOSIAH MORSE, brother of Deidama Morse Collin, resided in Hillsdale, N. Y., and died, 1802. By his last will and testament, executed June 7th, 1801, he bequeathed his estate to his wife, Mehitable, and his brothers Benjamin and Peter Morse, and his nephews, John and Josiah Morse, and to his friend, Charles Frederick; and he appointed his brother-in-law, John Collin, to be his executor. The witnesses to the will were, Charles Whitwood, Asa Alger and Thomas Andrews. The will was admitted to probate, July 14th, 1802, by W. W. Van Ness, Surrogate, before whom the executor, John Collin, duly qualified.

Capt. JOHN MORSE, father of Virginia Morse, and father-in-law of Leonidas Price Hamline, was born in Virginia, and died in California, January 12th, 1866.

THEODOSIA, wife of Capt. John Morse, was born in New Jersey. She had a daughter—Virginia,—born November 9th, 1835. She had been previously married to Dr. Rees, of Philadelphia, who died without children.

VIRGINIA MORSE, daughter of John and Theodosia Morse, was born at Ripley, Ohio, November 9th, 1835, and married to Leonidas Price Hamline, December 31st, 1850. Her children are :

Leonidas Morse, born October 5th, 1852.
John Henry, born March 23d, 1856.
Eliza, born February 6th, 1859; died February 26th, 1859.
Theodosia, born June 30th, 1862.
Virginia Melinda, born March 23d, 1866.

OTHNEIL MOSES, maternal grandfather of Leonidas Lent Hamline, was born on Long Island, N. Y., in 1728, and married to Sarah Pinny, of Windsor, Conn.; died in Burlington, 1816. He had eleven children, and served as a soldier in the French war, and as a captain in the war of the Revolution. His wife was born in Windsor, Conn., 1734; died in Burlington. Conn.. 1822. His children were: Othneil, Reuben, Elihu, Isaac, Polly, Dorcas, Roxany, Olive, Rhoda and Cynthia.

OTHNEIL MOSES, son of Othneil and Sarah Pinny Moses, born on Long Island, N. Y., and married Polly David, and settled in Burlington, Conn., where he died. He served as a captain in the war of the Revolution.

REUBEN MOSES, son of Othneil and Sarah Pinny Moses, born on Long Island, N. Y., and married Hannah Brooks. He was a soldier in the war of the Revolution.

ELIHU MOSES, son of Othneil and Sarah Pinny Moses, born in Burlington, Conn., and married Miss Brooks, and settled in Cleveland, Ohio, and served in the war of 1812, and was on board of Perry's fleet in the battle on lake Erie, and died in the lake, leaving a wife and four children.

ISAAC MOSES, son of Othneil and Sarah Pinny Moses, died in the Florida war.

SARAH MOSES, daughter of Othneil and Sarah Pinny Moses, married John Balch, and settled in New York city.

POLLY MOSES, daughter of Othneil and Sarah Pinny Moses, married Hezekiah Richards, of New Hartford Conn.

DORCAS MOSES, daughter of Othneil and Sarah Pinny Moses, married Joel Dorman, of Burlington, Conn.

ROXANY MOSES, daughter of Othneil and Sarah Moses, born in Burlington, Conn., 1767, and married to Mark Hamline. They were the parents of the Rev. Leonidas Lint Hamline.

OLIVE MOSES, daughter of Othneil and Sarah Pinny Moses, married Mr. Walker, and settled in Homer, N. Y.

RHODA MOSES, daughter of Othneil and Sarah Pinny Moses, married a German, who was subsequently lost at sea.

CYNTHIA MOSES, daughter of Othneil and Sarah Pinny Moses, married John Talbot, of Hartford county, Conn., and settled in Clarendon, Ohio; she died in 1856. The children of Othneil and Sarah Pinny Moses, with but two exceptions, lived to an advanced age, and were distinguished for piety, and the men for military services.

RACHAEL MOSES, sister of Othneil Moses, was born on Long Island, N. Y., and married to Mr. Wilcox, and settled in New Hartford, Conn. She was a woman of great fortitude; and during the French war, while her husband and sons were in the army, she rendered important services as nurse and physician to the inhabitants of her own and the adjoining towns.

ORVILLE McALPIN, son of John McAlpin, born in Hillsdale, November 29th, 1814, and married Lavina Becker, daughter of John P. and Elizabeth Clum Becker, January 1st, 1851. Their children were:

> Mary Caroline, born November 25th, 1851; died September, 1855.
> Lucy, born September 3d, 1857.

MARY CAROLINE McALPIN, daughter of Orville and Lavina Becker McAlpin, born November 25th, 1851, and died September 15th, 1855. She was a most amiable and interesting child, and intelligent above her years. And thus early passing to the grave, illustrates the adage, that Death loves a shining mark.

JOHN NOXON, of Great Barrington, Mass., married Nancy Johnson, daughter of Artemas and Susan Sherwood Johnson, and granddaughter of Hannah Collin Sherwood. They had one child, Joseph.

HIRAM NILES, of Connecticut, married Chloe Robinson, daughter of Gain and Chloe Bradish Robinson. They had one son and five daughters.

MATTHEW ORR, of Bridgwater, Mass., marrried Mary Robinson, daughter of James and Jerusha Bartlet Robinson, and moved to Nine Partners, Dutchess county, N. Y. After his decease, she moved to Palmyra, Wayne county, N. Y. Her children were: Margaret, Anna, John, James, Watson, and Corbet.

Margaret married John Stafford, of Rhode Island.

Anna married John Averil.

John and James went to Ohio.

Watson settled in Schoharie county, N. Y., and represented that county in the State Legislature in 1834.

Corbet Orr commanded a sloop on the Hudson river for some years.

DAVID ORR, of Bridgwater, Mass., married Elizabeth Corbet, a granddaughter of Gain and Margaret Watson Robinson, and moved to Nine Partners, Dutchess county, N. Y. After his decease she married John Vandusen of Hillsdale.

HUGH ORR, of Bridgwater, Mass., moved to Hillsdale, N. Y., and married Miss Heath.

ROBERT ORR resided in Hillsdale, and was brother of Matthew, David and Hugh Orr.

MARY OSBORN, daughter of Melvin Osborn, of Michigan, married David Lonson Becker, son of John P. and Elizabeth Clum Becker, and settled in Benton, Yates county, N. Y. She has one daughter, Lizzie.

HARRIET N. OSBORN, daughter of Melvin Osborn, of Michigan, born 1822, and married George Sornborger, of Hillsdale, died September 19th, 1871. Her children were: .

Mary, born August 11th, 1851; died April 1st, 1857.

Florence, born September 11th, 1855.

AVERY PARK, born in Preston, Conn., December 23d, 1781, and married Betsey Meech, September 14th, 1806, and settled in Burlington, Otsego county, N. Y., 1809. Their children are:

Roswell, born October 1st, 1807.

Daniel A., born September 13th, 1810.

Harriet, born March 3d, 1814.

Eliza, born October 13th, 1816.

Maria L., born March 13th, 1820.

Clarissa, born January 22d, 1822.

ROSWELL PARK, son of Avery and Betsey Meech Park, born October 1st, 1807, and married Mary B. Baldwin, December 28th, 1836. After her death, in October 23d, 1854, he married Elizabeth Niles, of Wisconsin, April 25th, 1860. He died July 16th, 1869. Roswell Park possessed poetic talents of a very high order, of which the following extract, written when only sixteen years of age, is an evidence :

When storms are uplifting the waves of the ocean,
  Or when the bright sunbeams enliven the day,
When nature inspires us with warmest emotion,
  We still think of kindred and friends far away.
When time has fled by and our absence is finished,
  To scenes of enjoyment we cheerfully come ;
And still our affection remains undiminished
  For much beloved kindred and thrice welcome home.

DANIEL A. PARK, son of Avery and Betsey Meech Park, born September 13th, 1810, and married Emeline E. Rhodes, January 1st, 1834.

HARRIET PARK, daughter of Avery and Betsey Meech Park, born March 3d, 1814, and married Russell G. Dorr, of Hillsdale, September 19th, 1832, by whom she has had two children, Martin H., and Harriet.

ELIZA PARK, daughter of Avery and Betsey Meech Park, born October 13th, 1816, and married Norton S. Collin, of Hillsdale, September 23d, 1837. Her children are :

Eliza, born February 27th, 1839.

Lucy, born February 21st, 1841.

Norton Park, born June 9th, 1842.

Virginia, born August 26th, 1851; died August, 1856.

Cardora, born May 10th, 1858.

MARIA L. PARK, daughter of Avery and Betsey Meech Park, born March 13th, 1820, and married Henry Clark Collin, of Benton, Yates county, N. Y. Her children are :

Henry Park, born July 26th, 1843.

Charles Avery, born May 18th, 1846.

Mary Louise, born June 7th, 1848.

Frederick, born August 2d, 1850.

Emeline, born February 16th, 1852.

George, born February 3d, 1854.

William Welch, born January 2d, 1856.

Frank McAlpin, born September 17th, 1859.

CLARISSA PARK, daughter of Avery and Betsey Meech Park, born January 22d, 1822, and married David Collin, son of David and Anna Smith Collin, October 22d, 1845, by whom she had nine children :

David, born January 6th, 1847 ; died November 3d, 1862.

Edward, born September 30th, 1848.

Clara Park, born May 25th, 1850.

Rosewell Park, born January 4th, 1852.

Charles Lee, born November 23d, 1853.

Harriett, born August 14th, 1856.

Miriam, born February 7th, 1859.

William Taylor, born March 28th, 1861.

Daniel Francis, born November 16th, 1863.

ELTWEED POMEROY, of Northampton, Massachusetts, died May 22d, 1662. His children were : Medad, Eldad, John, and Joseph.

MEDAD POMEROY, son of Eltweed Pomeroy, had a son, Ebenezer, who married Miss King, of Northampton, and their children were : John, Ebenezer, Sarah, Simeon, Jonah, Seth, Daniel, and Thankful.

SETH POMEROY, son of Ebenezer, and grand son of Deacon Medad Pomeroy, born at Northampton, Massachusetts, 1707, and married Miss Hunt ; died in the war of the Revolution, 1777, and was buried with the honors of war near the Baptist Church in Peekskill, N. Y. His children were : Seth, Quartus, Medad, Lemuel, Martha, Mary, Sarah, and Asahel.

He engaged, while quite young, in military duties, and was a captain in 1744, and a major at the capture of Louisburg in 1745. In 1755, he was lieutenant colonel in Williams' regiment, and was the chief commander in the bat - tle with the army of general Diskau. His regiment was most prominent, and suffered most in gaining the victory at Lake George. He was a delegate to the Provincial Congress in 1774 and 1775. In October 1774, he, with Preble and Ward, were chosen general officers ; and in February, 1775, a brigadier general. He was in the hot. test of the fight at Bunker's Hill, and a few days after was appointed senior brigadier general, and died in the army, 1777.

LEMUEL POMEROY, son of Seth Pomeroy, born 1737, was forty years a member of the State Legislature ; died at Southampton December, 1819.

QUARTUS POMEROY, son of general Seth Pomeroy, mar. ried and had five children : Thaddeus, George, Seth, Martha, and Hannah.

SETH POMEROY, son of Quartus Pomeroy, married Hannah Wells, and had seven children : Quartus Wells,

George Eltweed, Henry Brown, Louis Dwight, Thaddeus, Seth. Martha Whitlesey, and Mariah Ashman.

GEORGE ELTWEED POMEROY, son of Seth, and grandson of Quartus, and great grand son of general Seth Pomeroy, married Hellen E. Robinson, daughter of Gain and Chloe Bradish Robinson, and settled in Toledo, Ohio. Their children were : Two Hellen Augustas, Martha Hannah, Mary Jane, Maria Louise, George Eltweed, Mary Robinson, and Thaddeus. Of these, one Hellen Augusta, Mary Jane, and Thaddeus, are dead.

HELLEN AUGUSTA POMEROY, daughter of George Eltweed and Hellen E. Robinson Pomery, married Geo. S. Thorbun.

The POMEROYS descended from Sir Ralph de Pomeroy, a knight in the army of William the Conqueror, whom he accompanied to England, and for his distinguished services the King granted him fifty manors in Derbyshire, and several in Somersetshire, upon which he built a castle, which is still in tolerable preservation, and occupied by his descendants.

When the Earl of Essex was Lord Lieutenant of Ireland, one of the younger branches of the Pomeroy family accompanied him in the capacity of chaplain, and among his descendants is Major-General John Pomeroy, who served in the British army in America during the revolutionary war.

The branch from which all the Pomeroys in the United States descended, emigrated about the year 1635, and consisted of two brothers, Eltweed and Eldred, who first settled at Dorchester, near Boston.

DANIEL QUINCY, born in England, and emigrated to this country, settled in Boston and married Ann Shephard, daughter of the Rev. Thomas Shephard, of that town, and granddaughter of the Rev. Thomas Shephard, of Cambridge. He was a goldsmith by occupation, and died August 10th, 1690. He had two children, Ann and John.

Ann Quincy, daughter of Daniel and Ann Shephard Quincy, born in Boston, June 1st, 1685, and married Col. John Holman, of Milton, Mass., and settled in Bridgewater, Mass., where she died, leaving five children. John, Ann, Peggy, Ruth, and Mary. She was the great-grandmother of Ruth Holman Collin, of Hillsdale.

John Quincy, son of Daniel and Ann Shephard Quincy, born in Boston, July 21st, 1689. He graduated at Harvard University, 1708, and was for many years a member of the State Legislature and its speaker, and for several years a member of the council and a colonel in the militia. He died, July 13th, 1767, just two days after the birth of his celebrated great-grandson, John Quincy Adams, who, subsequently, inherited his estate. His daughter married the Rev. William Smith, of Weymouth, by whom she had two daughters, one of whom, Abigail, married ex-President John Adams, the other married Judge Crouch, of the United States court.

George Robbins, born in Lenox, Mass., and married Jane S. Collin, daughter of James and Jane B. Hunt Collin, October 28th, 1847, by whom he has had two children :

Mary E., born in Ohio.
James, born in New Marlborough, Mass.

Nicholas Race, born December 25th, 1739. His wife, Lucretia, was born December 12th, 1744. They settled in Egremont, Mass., and lived to very great age. Their children were: Andrew, Stephen, Abram, Rebecca, Isaac N., William, and others.

REBECCA RACE, daughter of Nicholas and Lucretia Race, born in Egremont, Mass., September, 1st, 1781, and married to Charles Tullar, son of Seneca and Eunice Tullar, of Egremont, November 27th, 1799; died in Sheffield, Mass., December 22d, 1861. Her children were:

Seneca Charles, born February 10th, 1801.
Tabitha Paulina, born March 16th, 1804.
Isaac R., born May 4th, 1806.
Pamelia Jane, born April 11th, 1808.
David W., born May, 31st, 1812.
Lucretia, born May 22d, 1816.
William Frederick, born June 12th, 1818.

GAIN ROBINSON, born in Scotland, 1682, and emigrated to Ireland, and married a wife, by whom he had two children, Archibald and Susan. His wife having died, he emigrated to this country and married Margaret Watson, and lived for a time in Braintree, Mass., and for a time at Pembroke, and finally settled in East Bridgewater. He had recommendations from the churches in Ireland, Braintree and Pembroke. He died, 1763. His children by his last marriage were:

Alexander.
Joseph.
Gain, born, 1724.
Increase, born, 1727.
Betty, born, 1728.
James, born, 1730.
John, born, 1732.
Margaret, born, 1735.
Mary, born, 1738.
Martha, born, 1740.
Jane, born, 1742.
Robert, born, 1746.

ARCHIBALD ROBINSON, son of Gain Robinson, born in Ireland, and emigrated to this country. He married Mercy Field, daughter of Richard Field, of Bridgewater, Mass., 1747, and had two sons:

Robert, born, 1747.
John, born, 1749.

SUSANNAH ROBINSON, daughter of Gain Robinson, born in Ireland, and emigrated to this country, and married Christopher Erskine.

ALEXANDER ROBINSON, son of Gain and Margaret Watson Robinson, born in Braintree, Mass., and married Hannah White, 1745, and had a daughter, Abigail, 1746, and moved to Nova Scotia.

JOSEPH ROBINSON, son of Gain and Margaret Watson Robinson, born, 1722, and married Abigail Keith, daughter of Joseph Keith, 1746. Their children were:

Joseph, born, 1747.
Benjamin, born, 1748.
Edward, born, 1750.
Susannah, born, 1753.
Abigail, born, 1755.

His wife, Abigail, having died, he married Hannah Snow, daughter of Isaac Snow, 1759. Their children were:

Isaac, born, 1760.
Hannah, born, 1763.
Snow, born, 1765.

Having died in 1766, his estate was settled by his brother James. His son, Snow, died in the revolutionary army, at West Point, 1783.

7

GAIN ROBINSON, son of Gain and Margaret Watson Robinson, born 1724, and married Miss Dyer; died in 1778. His children were: Gain, William, Increase, John, Dyer, born, 1765; Joseph, Ansel, Sally and Zibeah.

JAMES ROBINSON, son of Gain and Margaret Watson Robinson, born 1730, and married Jerusha Bartlet, daughter of Ebenezer Bartlet, of Duxbury, Mass. His children were : James and Bartlet, twins, Watson, Abner, Gain, Clark, Jerusha Bartlet, born 1753, Margaret, born 1754, Mary, Elizabeth, Jane, Esther, Bethia. Previous to 1775 he lived on Clark's Island, in Plymouth harbor. From thence he moved to Bridgewater, where he resided five years, and then moved to Cummington, Mass., where he died, 1793.

JAMES ROBINSON, son of James and Jerusha Bartlet Robinson, born 1750. He had a nautical education and had the command of a ship at an early age, and in his ship the first arms and military stores were brought from France at the commencement of the Revolutionary war. To get possession of some of the arms and munitions that he imported, brought on the first fight at Concord and Lexington, which roused the martial spirit of the nation. After the commencement of the war he left the ocean and took a command in the army and was at the battles of Bunker's Hill and those fought with the army of Burgoyne, and sat beside the death-bed of his brother Abner, who fell in one of those battles. He died himself in the army near the close of the war.

BARTLET ROBINSON, son of James and Jerusha Bartlet Robinson and twin brother of James Robinson, born 1750, and was with his brother on the ocean and most of the battles in the Revolutionary war, and died in the army.

WATSON ROBINSON, son of James and Jerusha Bartlet Robinson, born 1751, and married Anna Webster, of Goshen, Mass. He was in the battle of Bunker's Hill and served as a soldier through the war of the Revolution, and died in Palmyra, N. Y., leaving several children.

ABNER ROBINSON, son of James and Jerusha Bartlet Robinson, born 1761, and was killed in battle at Still-water, Saratoga county, N. Y., October, 1777. The circumstances attending his death are worthy of considera-tion. It was during the darkest period of the American revolution. The British arms had been uniformly success-ful, and to their final success it seemed only necessary to establish a line of fortified posts from New York to Canada, by way of the Hudson. To that end the army of Sir Henry Clinton had advanced from New York to Columbia county, and had burned the manor house of the Livingstons. The army of General Burgoyne had advanced from Canada to Saratoga county, and had burned the splendid mansion of General Schuyler. To prevent the junction of those armies, General Washington sent some of his best troops under the command of General Gates. Among those troops were the brothers James Bartlet and Watson Robinson. Those troops were joined by a volun-teer company from Bridgewater, Mass., under the command of Captain Jacob Allen, and in that company were Thomas Latham and Abner Robinson, boys of about sixteen years of age.

In October, 1777, those troops gave battle to the army of Gen. Burgoyne. During the fight it became advisable to withdraw that wing in which the Bridgewater company fought; and while retiring before a pressing enemy, firing by platoons with all the order of veterans, Capt. Allen fell and was borne from the field. Soon after young Rob-inson fell, mortally wounded, and the retiring troops were about to leave him, when his youthful companion stepped beside him. When admonished by his comrades that he would fall into the hands of the enemy, he replied, "This boy must be carried from the field, or I stay with him." This brought assistance, and Abner Robinson was in consequence permitted to die in his tent, with his brother James sitting beside him. This act of Thomas Latham has endeared the name to all who have in their veins the blood of the Robinsons.

„Brave boys! had I the genius of a Virgil, your names should be handed to posterity beside those of Nisus and Eurialus.

INCREASE ROBINSON, son of Gain and Margaret Watson Robinson, born 1727, and married Rachael Bates, of Hingham, Mass., 1755, and died in the French war, 1756. He was a Sergeant under Gen. Winslow.

MARY ROBINSON, daughter of Gain and Margaret Watson Robinson, born 1738, and married Richard Bartlet, 1757.

MARTHA ROBINSON, daughter of Gain and Margaret Watson Robinson, born 1740, and married Archibald Thompson, 1761.

JOHN ROBINSON, son of Gain and Margaret Watson Robinson, born 1732, and married Miss Studley. His daughter, Martha, married Eliphalet Bailey, 1782.

ROBERT ROBINSON, son of Gain and Margaret Watson Robinson, born 1746, and married Bethiah Kingman, 1772. Their children were: Samuel, James, and others. They settled in Cummington, Mass.

BENJAMIN ROBINSON, son of Joseph and Abigail Keith

Robinson, born 1748, and married Eve Packard, daughter of James Packard, 1770. Their children were :

Anna, born 1771.
Deborah, born 1777.
Susannah, born 1781.
Benjamin, born 1784.
Kilborn, born 1787.
Polly, born 1790.
Hodijah, born 1793.

His wife, Eve, died 1796, and he married Keziah, widow of Elijah Packard, and daughter of John Ames, 1798. Their children were :

Nabby Lazell, born 1799.
Bethiah Ames, born 1802.
Margaret Watson, born 1806.

He died 1829, and his wife, Keziah, died 1838.

ANNA ROBINSON, daughter of Benjamin and Eve Packard Robinson, born 1771, and married Uriah Brett, 1799.

DEBORAH ROBINSON, daughter of Benjamin and Eve Packard Robinson, born 1777, and married John Adams 1798.

SUSANNAH ROBINSON, daughter of Benjamin and Eve Packard Robinson, born 1781, and married Ichabod Keith 1802.

POLLY ROBINSON, daughter of Benjamin and Eve Packard Robinson, born 1790, and married Mr. Bradbury, of Maine, and after his decease she married a Mr. Herrick, of Boston.

NABBY LAZELL ROBINSON, daughter of Benjamin and Keziah Robinson, born 1799, and married Samuel P. Condon 1821 ; died 1832.

BETHIAH AMES ROBINSON, daughter of Benjamin and Keziah Robinson, born 1802, and married Martin Ramsdell.

MARGARET WATSON ROBINSON, daughter of Benjamin and Keziah, born 1806, and became the second wife of Samuel P. Condon.

WILLIAM ROBINSON, son of Gain and Miss Dyer Robinson. married Hannah Eggerton 1780 ; died 1816. Their children were :

> William, born 1784.
> Abigail, born 1786 ; died 1804.
> Marcus, born 1791.
> Sally, born 1795.
> Mary Hitchborn and Maria Dyer, twins, born 1799.

WILLIAM ROBINSON, son of William and Hannah Eggerton Robinson, born 1784, and married Abigail Delano, of Duxbury, 1812.

MARCUS ROBINSON, son of William and Hannah Eggerton Robinson, born 1791, and married Charlotte Barstow, of Pembroke, 1820.

SALLY ROBINSON, daughter of William and Hannah Eggerton Robinson, born 1795, and married Henry Gray.

MARY HITCHBORN ROBINSON, daughter of William and Hannah Eggerton Robinson, born 1799, and married James Sidall.

DYER ROBINSON, son of Dyer and Abigail Stetson Robinson, born 1792, and married Miss Standish.

GAD ROBINSON, son of Dyer and Abigail Stetson Robinson, born 1795, and married Margaret Orr Keith, 1821.

JACOB ROBINSON, son of Dyer and Abigail Stetson Robinson, born 1798, and married Rhoda W. Chandler. Their children were :

Caroline E., born 1823.
Jacob Harvey, born 1826.
Lydia Hall, born 1827.

CHARLES ROBINSON, son of Dyer and Abigail Stetson Robinson, married Ann Maria Keith.

SALOME ROBINSON, daughter of Dyer and Abigail Stetson Robinson, married Zenas Keith, 1821.

ABIGAIL ROBINSON, daughter of Dyer and Abigail Stetson Robinson, married Capt. Scott Keith.

CAPT. BENJAMIN ROBINSON, son of Benjamin and Eve Packard Robinson, born 1784, and married Mary Packard, 1809. Their children were : Benjamin Roseter, James Lawrence, Elijah Packard, born 1816 ; Mary, born 1818. Their son, James Lawrence, died at sea, 1835.

HODIJAH ROBINSON, son of Benjamin and Eve Packard Robinson, born 1793, and married Silvia Orr, daughter of Hugh Orr, and had one daughter, Lucia Watson Herbert.

GAIN ROBINSON, son of James and Jerusha Bartlet Robinson, born January 24th, 1771, and married Chloe Bradish, daughter of Col. John Bradish, of Cummington, Mass., 1796, and settled in Palmyra, N. Y. His children were : Amanda, William Cullen, Caius Cassius, Abigail Blackman, Clark, Erasmus Darwin, Charles Rollin, Chloe, Helen Elizabeth, and Margaret Sophia.

He was a man with talents of the first order, of fine appearance, of easy and gentlemanly address, and interesting in conversation, and distinguished as a physician. Died June 21st, 1832.

AMANDA ROBINSON, daughter of Gain and Chloe Bradish Robinson, born in Palmyra, Wayne county, N. Y., and married Philip Granden, by whom she has had eleven children; all now dead but two sons. Her son, William Granden, graduated at West Point.

WILLIAM CULLEN ROBINSON, son of Gain and Chloe Bradish Robinson, born in Palmyra, N. Y.; died in Illinois, unmarried.

CAIUS CASSIUS ROBINSON, son of Gain and Chloe Bradish Robinson, born in Palmyra, N. Y., and graduated at Fairfield, N. Y., Medical College, and moved to Palmyra, in Michigan. In the twenty-fourth year of his age he married Eliza Warner, daughter of Stephen Warner, of Cummington, Mass., and had one son, Lucius Gain, and died in the thirty-sixth year of his age.

ABIGAIL BLACKMAN ROBINSON, daughter of Gain and Chloe Bradish Robinson, born in Palmyra, N. Y., and married Alexander B. Tiffany, an attorney, who settled in Palmyra, Michigan, and became distinguished in his profession, and was raised to the bench. She had a large family of children, of whom only three are living—two daughters and one son.

CLARK ROBINSON, son of Gain and Chloe Bradish Robinson, born in Palmyra, N. Y., and married Delia Strong, by whom he had one daughter, Mary.

ERASMUS DARWIN ROBINSON, son of Gain and Chloe Bradish Robinson, born in Palmyra, N. Y., and married Calista Peck, and had three children, all now deceased. He settled, and now lives, in White Pigeon, Michigan.

CHARLES ROLLIN ROBINSON, son of Gain and Chloe Bradish Robinson, born in Palmyra, N. Y., and married Calista

Corbett, and had one daughter, now deceased. He settled and cultivated a farm in Palmyra, Michigan.

CHLOE ROBINSON, daughter of Gain and Chloe Bradish Robinson, born in Palmyra, N. Y., and married Hiram Niles, of Connecticut, and has had one son and five daughters.

CLARK ROBINSON, son of James and Jerusha Bartlet Robinson, born in Clark's Island, in Plymouth Harbor, Mass., and died in Cummington, Mass.

MARGARET SOPHIA ROBINSON, daughter of Gain and Chloe Bradish Robinson, born in Palmyra, N. Y., and married John E. Gavit, November 28th, 1840, and settled in Old Stockbridge, Mass. He is distinguished as an engraver, and has long been employed by the Government of the United States in that important capacity. She has had nine children, four sons and five daughters :

John, born August 4th, 1841; died a few months after.
Joseph, born December 22d, 1842.
Margaret, born March 22d, 1845.
William Edmonds, born February 10th, 1848.
Hellen Elizabeth, born November 26th, 1849.
Clark, born June 27th, 1851.
Julia Niles, born February 22d, 1854.
Chloe, born April 29th, 1856.
Pauline, born February 3d, 1859.

JERUSHA BARTLET ROBINSON, daughter of James and Jerusha Bartlet Robinson, born in Plymouth, 1753, and married Wait Wadsworth, of Duxbury, Mass., and settled there, where some of her descendants yet live.

MARGARET ROBINSON, daughter of James and Jerusha Bartlet Robinson, born in Plymouth, Mass., 1754, and married Elijah Fay, and settled in Hamilton, Madison county, N. Y., and they both died there, leaving a son James, who remained on the homestead and raised a numerous family. He married Morilla Nash, of that town.

MARY ROBINSON, daughter of James and Jerusha Bartlet Robinson, married Matthew Orr, and moved to the Nine Partners, in Dutchess county, N. Y. After the death of her husband, she moved to Palmyra, Wayne county, N. Y., where she died. Among her children were Watson, Corbett, Margaret, Anna, John, and Jonas.

ELIZABETH ROBINSON, daughter of James and Jerusha Bartlet Robinson, married Alexander McIntyre, and had three sons, Alexander, Thomas, and Abner. Her son Alexder became a distinguished physician, and died July 22d, 1859, leaving three children—a daughter and two sons.

ESTHER ROBINSON, daughter of James and Jerusha Bartlet Robinson, married Amos King, and settled in Hadley, Mass., where they died. Among their children (Warrener, whose recent death received honorable notice in the Springfield *Republican*), they had also a daughter, Minerva, who married Willard Nash, and settled in Madison county, N. Y.

ELEANOR ROBINSON, daughter of James and Jerusha Bartlet Robinson, married Jacob Convers. Among her children is a son, Maxey, who resides in Elmira, N. Y.

BETHIA ROBINSON, daughter of James and Jerusha Bartlet Robinson, born in Bridgewater, Mass., and married Charles Bradish, son of John and Hannah Warner Bradish, of Cummington, Mass., 1804, and moved to Palmyra, Wayne county, N. Y., 1807, where they died at advanced ages. Their children were: Alexander H., William F., Seth W., Bartlet R., Lucretia E., and Philander.

JANE ROBINSON, daughter of James and Jerusha Bartlet Robinson, born in Plymouth, Mass., August 6th, 1763, and married William Johnson, son of Benjamin and Ruth Holman Johnson, of Bridgewater, Mass., November 8th, 1779; died in Hillsdale, N. Y., April 7th, 1836. Her children were :

> Ruth Holman, born September 16th, 1780.
> Sophia, born January 7th, 1784.
> Melinda, born December 7th, 1785; died March 9th, 1792.
> Clynthia, born April 7th, 1788.
> Quincy, born April 5th, 1791.
> Melinda, born September 29th, 1801.

AMELIA ANN ROBBINS, born November 29th, 1799, and married Theodore W. Whiting, March 15th, 1820, by whom she had two children :

> Harriet Amelia, born December 10th, 1821.
> Frederick Theodore, born June 6th, 1825.

GEORGE ROBBINS, born in Lenox, Mass., and married Jane S. Collin, daughter of James and Jane B. Hunt Collin, and settled in New Marlborough, Mass. They have had two children : Mary E., and James.

NATHAN SEWARD, of New Hartford, N. Y., born November 28th, 1814, and married Harriette Collin, daughter of David and Anna Smith Collin, June 13th, 1848. Their children were :

> Harriette, born March 19th, 1849.
> Anna, born May 26th, 1850.
> Nathan, born November 24th, 1851 ; died November 28th, 1851.
> Lucy, born July 17th, 1853.
> Elizabeth, born February 13th, 1855 ; died April 13th, 1855.

EMELINE SORNBORGER, daughter of Uriah Sornborger, born November 19th, 1820, and married William Leonard Johnson, son of Quincy and Abigail Cook Johnson, September 12th, 1852. Their children were :

Ida, born September 10th, 1853 ; died April 24th, 1856.

Willie, born September 13th, 1855 ; died September 25th, 1855.

Franklin, born June 2d, 1857.

George Quincy, born December 5th, 1859.

GEORGE SORNBORGER, son of Uriah Sornborger, born 1820, and married Harriet N. Osborn, daughter of Melvin Osborn, 1852. Their children were :

Mary, born August 11th, 1853 ; died September 1st, 1857.

Florence, born September 11th, 1855.

ARIEL SMITH, of West Stockbridge, Mass., married and had a daughter, Olive. After the death of his wife he married Rebecca, widow of Charles Tullar, and daughter of Nicholas and Lucretia Race. He was a respectable member of the Baptist Church, and died in West Stockbridge.

LUCY SMITH, of Dutchess county, N. Y., married David Collin, son of John and Hannah Merwin Collin, February 19th, 1764 ; died March 15th, 1767. Her children were :

Hannah, born 1765.

David, born February 22d, 1767.

ANNA SMITH, of Dutchess county, N. Y., married David Collin, son of David and Lucy Bingham Collin, January 2d, 1817. Her children were :

Edmund, born December 28th, 1817 ; died December 29th, 1817.

Caroline, born December 26th, 1818.
Lucy B., born March 15th, 1821.
David, born August 23d, 1822.
Harriett, born November 15th, 1824.
Miriam, born May 16th, 1828.
Anna Smith, born October 4th, 1829.

LYDIA SMITH, of Amenia, Dutchess county, N. Y., married Lee Collin, son of David and Lucy Bingham Collin, by whom she had one child.

ELY SMITH, of Bridgeport, Conn., married Huldah Merwin, daughter of Miles and Mary Brewster Merwin. Their children were, Almon, Mary, and Ruth.

PORTER TREMAIN, son of Augustus Tremain, of Hillsdale, N. Y., married Amanda Collin, daughter of David and Lucy Bingham Collin, November 11th, 1830, by whom he had one son, Augustus, born March 27th, 1834. After the death of his wife, Amanda, on March 26th, 1840, he married Lucy B. Collin, daughter of David and Anna Smith Collin, September 28th, 1841, by whom he had two sons :

Charles, born April 23d, 1843.
Porter, born January 24th, 1852.

JOHN TRUESDELL, born July 1st, 1722, and married Rachel Wright, September, 1743 ; died February 1st, 1782. His children were :

Hannah, born August 24th, 1744.
David, born September 2d, 1749.
Stephen, born June 10th, 1753.
John, born May 11th, 1755.

After the death of his wife, Rachel, he married Sarah Sneadwell, November 7th, 1757, by whom he had one son, Thomas, born February 2d, 1759.

THOMAS TRUESDELL, son of John and Sarah Sneadwell Truesdell, born February 2d, 1759, and married Hannah Collin, daughter of. John and Sarah Arnold Collin, September 3d, 1781 ; died at Wilmington, Ohio, April 10th, 1822. His children were :

John W., born May 7th, 1783.
Bebee, born January 10th, 1784.
Sarah, born June 17th, 1785.
Harry, born March 1st, 1788.
James, born September 3d, 1790 ; died October 12th, 1790.
Arnold, born September 15th, 1796.
Gove, born May 14th, 1802; died January 30th, 1818.

JOHN W. TRUESDELL, son of Thomas and Hannah Collin Truesdell, born May 7th, 1783, and married to Anna Esmond, daughter of Isaiah Esmond, July 25th, 1804 ; died September 23d, 1806. His children were :

Bebee, born June 5th, 1805 ; died April, 1811.
John W., born November 13th, 1806.

SARAH TRUESDELL, daughter of Thomas and Hannah Collin Truesdell, born June 17th, 1785, and married Erastus Tactor, of Ontario county, N. Y., March 11th, 1804 ; died May 17th, 1810. Her husband died January 7th, 1813. Their children were :

Hannah, born March 19th, 1805.
Lydia, born June 10th, 1807.
Sarah, born June 30th, 1809.

HARRY TRUESDELL, son of Thomas and Hannah Collin Truesdell, born March 1st, 1788, and married Clynthia Johnson, daughter of William and Jane Robinson Johnson, February 19th, 1809 ; died October 14th, 1844. His children were :

Arnold Fletcher, born January 6th, 1810.
Sarah Madeline, born May 12th, 1812.
John Quincy, born February 22d, 1825.

BEBEE TRUESDELL, son of Thomas and Hannah Collin
Truesdell, born January 10th, 1794, and married Margaret
Post, December 10th, 1815 ; died at Wilmington, Ohio,
1866. His children were :

John Osmond, born October 3d, 1811.
Aurelia A. A. E., born December 24th, 1817.
C. Fernando, born February 16th, 1820.
Charles Seymour, born December 31st, 1822 ; died
    April 4th, 1823.
Anna Maria, born August 21st, 1824.

ARNOLD TRUESDELL, son of Thomas and Hannah Collin
Truesdell, born September 15th, 1796, and married Melinda
Johnson, daughter of William and Jane Robinson Johnson,
September 10th, 1820; died at Wilmington, Ohio, March
28th, 1835, and was buried in the cemetery in Lebanon,
Ohio, in the family plot of the Rev. John and Lorania P.
Collin Braden.

GOVE TRUESDELL, son of Thomas and Hannah Collin
Truesdell, born May 14th, 1802; died January 30th, 1818.

ARNOLD FLETCHER TRUESDELL, son of Harry and Clynthia Johnson Truesdell, born January 6th, 1810, and married Chloe Bushnell, daughter of John and Loxey Lay
Bushnell. His children are : Morania, Julia, Emma, and
Madeline.

SARAH MADELINE TRUESDELL, daughter of Harry and
Clynthia Johnson Truesdell, born in Hillsdale, and mar-
ried Seymour Foster, son of Parla and Phebe Wells Foster.
Her children were : Wells, Henrietta, Augustus, and Willie.

JOHN QUINCY TRUESDELL, son of Harry and Clynthia Johnson Truesdell, born February 22d, 1825, and married Julia Ann Hollenbeck, February 14th, 1843. His children are :

    Harry, born December 20th, 1843.
    Clynthia Augusta, born July 15th, 1845.
    Arnold F., born April 25th, 1848.
    George Emmet, born June 11th, 1851.
    Marion Darwin, born December 9th, 1857.
    Elmer Quincy, born November 23d, 1861.

HARRY TRUESDELL, son of John Quincy and Julia Ann Hollenbeck Truesdell, born December 20th, 1843, and married Ellen Minkler, July 4th, 1867.

CLYNTHIA AUGUSTA TRUESDELL, daughter of John Quincy and Julia Ann Hollenbeck Truesdell, born July 15th, 1845, and married Philip Becker, son of Philip and Elizabeth DeGraff Becker, July 15th, 1866. Their children are :

    Julia, born April, 1867.
    Gordon, born September 9th, 1868.

GEORGE EMMET TRUESDELL, son of John Quincy and Julia Ann Hollenbeck Truesdell, born June 11th, 1851 ; died July 18th, 1861.

GAINS TRUESDELL, son of Samuel Truesdell, born in Hillsdale, and married Polly Becker, daughter of John P. and Betsy Clum Becker. His children are : John, Stephen, Ruth, Elizabeth, and Juliette.

ARNOLD F. TRUESDELL, son of John Quincy and Julia Ann Hollenbeck Truesdell, born April 25th, 1848 ; married Adda Slater.

SENECA TULLAR, born June 21st, 1751. His wife, Eunice, was born August 2d, 1750. They settled in South Egremont, Mass., and lived to a great age. Their children were :

Charles, born June 3d, 1778, and Tabitha.

TABITHA TULLAR, daughter of Seneca and Eunice Tullar, of South Egremont, Mass., married Isaace N. Race, son of Nicholas and Lucretia Race. Her children were : Eunice, Seneca, Gorton, and others.

CHARLES TULLAR, son of Seneca and Eunice Tullar, born in South Egremont, Mass., June 3d, 1778, and married Rebecca Race, daughter of Nicholas and Lucretia Race; died August 26th, 1824. His children were :

Seneca C., born February 10th, 1801.
Tabitha Paulina, born March 16th, 1804.
Isaac R., born May 4th, 1806.
Pamelia Jane, born April 11th, 1808.
David W.. born May 31st, 1812.
Lucretia, born May 22d, 1815.
William Frederick, born June 12th, 1818.

SENECA C. TULLAR, son of Charles and Rebecca Race Tullar, born in South Egremont, February 10th, 1801, and married Mary A. Gordon, of Sheffield, who was born September 24th, 1804. They were married Sept. 30th, 1824. Their children were :

Charles A., born October 9th, 1825.
Pamelia Jane, born August 4th, 1828.
Rocelia Jennett, born July 7th, 1831.

CHARLES A. TULLAR, son of Seneca C. and Mary A. Gordon Tullar, born October 9th, 1825, and married Lucretia E. Church, November 10th, 1844; died October 22d, 1855.

PAMELIA JANE TULLAR, daughter of Seneca C. and

Mary A. Gordon Tullar, born August 4th, 1828, and married Silas L. Church, December 26th, 1851. Their children are :

Minnesota, born April 17th, 1853.
Virginia, born June 17th, 1859.

Rocelia Jennett Tullar, daughter of Seneca C. and Mary A. Gordon Tullar, born July 7th, 1831, and married Dyer Wait, March 27th, 1856. They have one son— Charles T.,—born January 1st, 1861.

Tabitha Paulina Tullar, daughter of Charles and Rebecca Race Tullar, born March 16th, 1804, and married John M. Bartholomew, of Sheffield, Mass., October 8th, 1822, by whom she has had two children :

Charles Willis, born September 14th, 1825.
Pamelia Jane, born December 28th, 1827.

Pamelia Jane Tullar, daughter of Charles and Rebecca Race Tullar, born April 11th, 1808, and married John F. Collin, son of John and Ruth Holman Johnson Collin, September 23d, 1827; died June 8th, 1870. Her children were :

Jane Paulina, born 1828; died September, 1830.
Hannah Clynthia, born 1829; died March, 1831.
Pamelia Laurania, born 1831.
John Frederick, born 1833.
Quincy Johnson, born 1836.
Frances Amelia, born 1840.

David W. Tullar, son of Charles and Rebecca Race Tullar, born May 31st, 1812, and married Laura L. Noteware, of Sheffield, Mass., June 7th, 1843. Their children were:

Susan Paulina, born March, 19th, 1844.
John F., born January 31st, 1846.

Lucretia Tullar, daughter of Charles and Rebecca Race Tullar, born May 22d, 1815, and married Freeman Van Dusen, of Hillsdale, 1837. Their children are:

Camilla Eugenia, born January 1st, 1842.
Paulina and Pamelia, twins, born October 6th, 1844.

William Frederick Tullar, son of Charles and Rebecca Race Tullar, born June 12th, 1818, and married Elizabeth Church, November 25th, 1841. She died July 6th, 1842, and he married Melinda French, October 16th, 1845, by whom he has one daughter :

Attie E., born April 4th, 1854.

John F. Tullar, son of David W. and Laura L. Noteware Tullar, born January 31st, 1846, and married to Mary Daly, who was born 1856.

Susan Paulina Tullar, daughter of David W. and Laura L. Noteware Tullar, born March 15th, 1844, and married Albert M. Williams, April 5th, 1862. Their children are:

Charlotte L., born March 7th, 1863.
Edson E., born October, 19th, 1868.

Walter B. Ten Broeck, born in Hillsdale, February 2d, 1827, and married Mary Ette Van Dusen, January 25th, 1855. Their children are:

Vandell, born January 16th, 1856.
Alice, born April 17th, 1859; died July 4th, 1861.
Jay W., born August 24th, 1861.
Carrie, born January 20th, 1863.

Seymour Van Dusen, born November 26th, 1810, and married Caroline McArthur, who was born May 11th, 1814. Their children are:

Mary Ette, born February 15th, 1835.
Jennett, born July 8th, 1837.
Delila, born August 12th, 1840.
Almira, born April 16th, 1842.
Annie, born September 1st, 1844.
Newton J., born November 8th, 1846.
Elizabeth, born March 5th, 1848.

MARY ETTE VAN DUSEN, daughter of Seymour and Caro. line McArthur Van Dusen, born February 15th, 1835, and married Walter B. Ten Broeck, January 25th, 1855. Their children are:

Vandell, born January 16th, 1856.
Alice, born April 17th, 1859; died July 4th, 1861.
Jay W., born August 24th, 1861.
Carrie, born January 20th, 1863.

JENNETT VAN DUSEN, daughter of Seymour and Caroline McArthur Van Dusen, born July 8th, 1837, and married John Frederick Collin, son of John F. and Pamelia Jane Tullar Collin, December 15th, 1857. Their children were:

John Jay, born December 12th, 1858; died July 2d, 1861.
Ruth Anna, born February 4th, 1863; died October 16th, 1870.
Frances Pamelia, born August 13th, 1866.

DELILA VAN DUSEN, daughter of Seymour and Caroline McArthur Van Dusen, born August, 1840, and married Ezra Best, and settled in Egremont, Mass.

ALMIRA VAN DUSEN, daughter of Seymour and Caroline McArthur Van Dusen, born April 16th, 1842, and married James Bain, of Copake.

ANNIE VAN DUSEN, daughter of Seymour and Caroline McArthur Van Dusen, born September 1st, 1844, and married Henry Hollenbeck, of Egremont; died September 25th, 1870, leaving one child.

NEWTON J. VAN DUSEN, son of Seymour and Caroline McArthur Van Dusen, born November 8th, 1846, and is now a telegraph operator at Ketonah, on the New York and Harlem Railroad.

ELIZABETH VAN DUSEN, daughter of Seymour and Caroline McArthur Van Dusen, born March 5th, 1848, and married Frank Clemens, of Ansonia, Conn., 1871.

FREEMAN VAN DUSEN, born February 7th, 1806, and married Lucretia Tullar, 1837. His children are : Cornelia Eugenia, born January 10th, 1842, Pamelia and Paulena, twins, born October 6th, 1844.

CAMELLA EUGENIA VAN DUSEN, daughter of Freeman and Lucretia Tullar Van Dusen, born January 1st, 1842, and married Edward Wills Blackington, of Adams, Mass., October 1st, 1862.

PAMELIA VAN DUSEN, daughter of Freeman and Lucretia Tullar Van Dusen, born October 6th, 1844, and married Albert H. Willis, October 5th, 1870.

PAULINA VAN DUSEN, daughter of Freeman and Lucretia Tullar Van Dusen, born October 5th, 1844, and married Edward C. Saxton, November 9th, 1869.

BARNET WAGER, son of John and Mary Arnold Wager, born January 29th, 1793, and married Lucy Collin, daughter of David and Lucy Bingham Collin; died April 15th, 1845.

MARGARET WATSON, born 1700, and married Gain Robinson, who settled in East Bridgwater, Mass. She died 1777. Her children were : Alexander, Joseph, Gain, Increase, Betty, James, John, Margaret, Mary, Martha, Jane, and Robert.

DYER WAIT, born June 5th, 1824, and married Rocelia Jennett Tullar, daughter of Seneca C. and Mary A. Gordon Tullar, March 27th, 1856, by whom he has had one child, Charles T., born January 1st, 1861.

SAMUEL JAMES WELLS, of New Hartford, N. Y., married Anna Smith Collin, daughter of David and Anna Smith Collin, October 12th, 1854, by whom he has had four children :

Samuel James, born September 5th, 1856.
David, born September 23d, 1858.
John Lewis, born December 26th, 1860.
Paul Irving, born March 9th, 1863.

FREDERICK T. WHITING, born June 6th, 1825, and married Ruth Maria Hill, daughter of Rodney and Sarah A. Collin Hill, December 11th, 1849. His children were :

John Fred, born December 13th, 1852.
Mary Anna, born July 12th, 1859.
Henry Mason, born February 10th, 1863.
Florence Amelia, born October 6th, 1869; died ——.

THEODORE W. WHITING, born April 8th, 1799, and married Amelia Ann Robbins, March 15th, 1820, by whom he had two children :

Harriet Amelia, born December 10th, 1821.
Frederick Theodore, born June 6th, 1825.

BENTLEY WHITE, of Connecticut, married Rhoda How, March 3d, 1819. His children were:

Sarah Ann, born January 14th, 1820.
Sibyl M., born May 29th, 1822; died December 18th, 1824.
Stephen, born March 17th, 1826.
Jane M., born October 20th, 1832; died October 20th, 1834.

STEPHEN WHITE, son of Bentley and Rhoda How White, born May 29th, 1822, and married Olive N. Chapman, October 26th, 1853. Their children are:

Mary L., born September 17th, 1854.
Ida M., born January 17th, 1856.
Bentley, born October 28th, 1857.
Ernest, born February 9th, 1860.
Helen M., born October 28th, 1866.

HIRAM H. WHITE, born in Canton, Conn., 1806, and married Jane M. Collin, daughter of John and Ruth Holman Johnson Collin, June 2d, 1830; died October 11th, 1864. He was a clergyman—a member of the New England Conference of the Methodist Episcopal Church, in which he labored for many years. In talents, integrity and eloquence, he had but few superiors.

SARAH ANN WHITE, daughter of Bentley and Rhoda How White, born January 14th, 1820, and married Henry A. Collin, son of John and Ruth Holman Johnson Collin, October 29th, 1836. Her children are:

Henry Alonzo, born August 14th, 1837.
Sarah Adeline, born January 3d, 1840.
Edwin, born August 31st, 1842.

BARAK WILSON, of Dutchess county, N. Y., married

Cordelia Collin, daughter of James and Lydia Hamblin Collin, September 21st, 1840; died March 26th, 1855.

ALBERT M. WILLIAMS, born at Stockbridge, Mass., August 31st, 1837, and married Susan Paulina Tullar, daughter of David W. and Laura L. Noteware Tullar, April 5th, 1862. His children are :

    Charles L., born March 7th, 1863.
    Edson E., born October 19th, 1868.

THERON WILSON, born June 10th, 1805, and married Lydia Louisa Collin, daughter of James and Lydia Hamblin Collin, January 8th, 1829; died January 27th, 1862. His children were :

    James, born June 17th, 1830.
    Eli Newton, born June 27th, 1832.
    George Theron, born February 3d, 1837.
    Sarah Louisa, born September 20th, 1834.
    Lydia Esther, born November 25th, 1840.
    Robert Hamblin, born November 23d, 1850.

ALBERT H. WILLIS, married Pamelia Van Dusen, daughter of Freeman and Lucretia Tullar Van Dusen, October 5th, 1870.

WORCESTER WHEELER, born December 28th, 1779, and married Wait Freeman; died May 7th, 1866. His children were :

    John T., born August 9th, 1818.
    Erastus, born January 7th, 1820.
    Louisa, born January 12th, 1822.
    Sarah A., born April 16th, 1824.
    Mary A., born October 22d, 1826.
    Charlotte A., born March 31st, 1829; died January 5th, 1866.
    Noah W., born March 30th, 1828.

LOUISA WHEELER, daughter of Worcester and Wait Freeman Wheeler, born January 12th, 1822, and married James Hamblin Collin, son of James and Lydia Hamblin Collin, September 11th, 1845.

SARAH A. WHEELER, daughter of Worcester and Wait Freeman Wheeler, born April 16th, 1824, and married Lewis S. Peck, September 7th, 1847.

MARY A. WHEELER, daughter of Worcester and Wait Freeman Wheeler, born October 22d, 1826, and married Isaac M. Vail, September 3d, 1844.

NOAH W. WHEELER, son of Worcester and Wait Freeman Wheeler, born March 30th, 1828, and married Sarah E. Bushnell, May, 1863 ; died August 7th, 1866.

LEWIS WRIGHT, born in Brunswick county, Virginia, February, 11th, 1796, and married Hannah Springer, of Uniontown, Pennsylvania, July 15th, 1823, by whom he had one daughter, Mary Elizabeth, born April 17th, 1824. His wife, Hannah Springer, died July 5th, 1827, and on the 16th of April, 1833, he married Hannah Collin, daughter of John and Ruth Holman Johnson Collin, by whom he had one daughter, Melinda T. He died November 8th, 1866.

MARY ELIZABETH WRIGHT, daughter of Lewis and Hannah Springer Wright, born April 17th, 1824, and married James H. Collin, son of James and Jane Hunt Collin, July 12th, 1843. Her children are : Frances M., Sarah M., Emma S., Henry Clay, and Jennie L.

MELINDA TRUESDELL WRIGHT, daughter of Lewis and Hannah Collin Wright, born March 27th, 1834, and married William A. Hanley, November 27th, 1857. Her children are :

Mariclin, born **August 16th, 1859.**
John Collin, born November 30th, 1861.
William Alonzo, born December 12th, 1865.
Louis Wright, born November 2d, 1862.

CHASTINE E. WOLVERTON, born at Charleston, Montgomery county, N. Y., July 12th, 1821, and married James Collin, son of John and Ruth Holman Johnson Collin, September 7th, 1847. Her children are :

Edwin W., born September 19th, 1849; died 1871.
Mortimer and Montcath, twins, born December 9th, 1852.
George W., born December 13th, 1855.
Hattie May, born May 1st, 1856.
Lizzie A., born March 12th, 1860.

APPENDIX.

———••———

THE declaration in the foregoing work, "that the influences that conceived such laws as the tariff of 1842, had produced the imputed cause which formed the excuse for provoking the late civil war," may provoke the criticisms of politicians and excite the incredulity of many honest men; therefore, for the instruction of the latter, the writer will, at a future time, write the history of those laws.

To say that the converting of West India molasses into Boston rum was one of the most cherished interests in New England, would excite almost universal incredulity; and yet that it is so, is a fact susceptible of the most positive proof. Over sixty thousand hogsheads of that West India molasses, with the aid of narcotics and water, are annually converted into over one hundred thousand hogsheads of that Boston rum. That rum has almost without exception been the material for procuring all slaves imported from Africa. It has been used to debase civilization and to make barbarians still more barbarous. It has produced many of the worst evils in this country, and, in fact, has been more mischievous to the world than any other occurrence since the fall of Adam. Yet it has been made the recipient of government bounties, and is now exempted from the taxation imposed upon other interests. To keep the people in ignorance, this Boston rum has been studiously excluded from every census except that of 1850.

The same wicked influences that have made Boston rum a cherished interest, is now operating in the perpetuation of the misnomer, a protective tariff. And the apparent controversy between the two Houses of Congress is only intended to deceive the people, and keep from them the fact that its effects are to make the great mass of the people slaves to a pampered aristocracy.

To create a debt as an excuse for imposing a high tariff upon which discriminations might be made for the benefit of the pampered few, was one of the objects for which the civil war was provoked. Had those pampered interests been taxed in proportion to others, that debt would now have been paid, and the object of the war would to them have been lost.

To avoid such payment, that debt is now being funded so as to make its payment impossible till a very remote period, without a breach of national faith to the public creditor. To pay the interest on such debt will of course perpetuate the existence of that aristocracy by a continuance of the high discriminating tariff, and to reconcile the people to this, they inculcate the doctrine that a national debt is a national blessing. Loyalty now consists in subserviency to those interests of Boston rum, discriminating tariff, and national debt. And to enforce that loyalty, the mailed hand is now upon the throats of a large portion of the people, and national liberty is gasping beneath the feet of a tyranny.